Getting Away With Murder

By the same Author

**Novels available in Amazon Paperback
under the name AJ Harper**

Liza Gray Dublin Detective - Book One
Liza Gray Dublin Detective - Book Two
Liza Gray Dublin Detective - Book Three
Liza Gray Dublin Detective - Book Four

What Goes Around
The Best Laid Plans
A Life Enjoyed
The Coffee Rooms

**Novels available in Amazon Paperback
under the name Alan Harper**

The Project
Getting Away With Murder

**Poetry available in Amazon Paperback
under the name Alan Harper**

Feathers on the Sea – Book 1
Feathers on the Sea – Book 2
Feathers on the Sea – Book 3
Feathers on the Sea – Book 4

**Other Books available in Amazon Paperback
under the name AJH**

Reflections
Christmas Dinner – A plan to be getting on with

Getting Away With Murder

By
Alan Harper

2001

This book is dedicated to Grainne Walsh

Chapter 1

I hadn't seen the guy for about two years.

Why I even stopped to talk to him was a bit of a mystery to me afterwards.

But there y'are. I did, and the rest, as they say, is history. A history never to be told in the completeness that is probably its due, but this is the nearest anybody will ever get to it.

It was a Saturday afternoon and I was after going up the Rathmines Road to the Swan Shopping Centre. There wasn't a thing to eat in the flat and I was hungry.

"Dunnes Stores" I thought, "And a bit of shopping."

Hangover and all, I put on a pair of jeans and a sweatshirt, and headed out the door to face the daylight. The sun was hard on my eyes and I didn't see anybody in the flurry of people on the way into Swan. It was as if I was still asleep and sleepwalking along the mall with my eyes closed.

Just as I got to the entrance of Dunnes I was rudely awoken by a slap on the shoulder and a welcome that was almost obscene in its cheerfulness. Groggily I saw Bert in front of me, a smile on his face that actually lifted my mood with a pleasant jolt.

"Well, hello stranger. Long time no see."

He had said the words and woken me up without anything actually registering for me. Like a moron I struggled for a suitable response to a question I hadn't comprehended and before my brain clicked into gear he was talking again.

"D'ye fancy a pint? Ye look like you could do with a cure. Let's head over to Slattery's".

Half-wittedly, I nodded and followed him out of the shopping centre. I wasn't even operating on autopilot. I was being sucked along in the slipstream of energy, only vaguely aware of my surroundings.

Slattery's, for a Saturday afternoon, was pretty busy. The sun shone lazily through the windows, giving the place a comfortable welcoming feel about itself. I edged my way through the buzz of people, vaguely aware of Bert a few steps ahead of me, a beacon giving me direction. He found two stools at the far end of the bar, and before I knew it he had two pints ordered and I was staring him in the face, unable to put two words together.

Clicking into autopilot I cranked up a grin. "So what have you been up to, ye owl devil?" I said.

He paid for the drinks and set the two pints of Guinness in front of us on the bar. "Time enough for that," he said, "Give me a minute to go to the bog. I'll be back before the pints settle."

I saw him work his way through the crowd and focused on the settling pints.

The first sip was heaven, the coppery taste cooling in my mouth and sliding graciously down my throat. I had about a quarter of the pint gone by the time he returned and I was sufficiently revived to see him coming down the pub with that buoyant grin on his face.

In the twenty seconds it took him to get to his stool and settle his arse on it I had the complete re-run of our past flash through my mind. My mind struggled to handle the mixed feelings the memories evoked.

The sudden moves from groggy hangover to pleasant recognition were hardly a suitable preparation for the sickening spin of emotions churning up in the pit of my stomach. But luckily my body was still moving slow enough for the reaction not to register on my face.

Bert had been my seatmate for a year at junior school when we were both about six. We'd both come from Limerford, a small town down the back end of nowhere, where everybody knew everybody else and knew a lot more besides about most of the inhabitants. In that world there was a mountain of knowledge hidden in the whispers behind closed doors, but even these whispers were the subject of rumour and gossip.

Back seventeen years ago, Bert and I had started school together. We used sit in the big heavy old wooden two seater desks that were made of cast iron and big slabs of good, hard wearing, wood. There was no lifty up tops that were a feature of the secondary school single seater jobbies.

I learnt very early on that Bert had a hidden streak in him.

Each of us had a little compartment under the desktop, a six inch high slot, into which we were supposed to put our bags, or books, or whatever, while we were industriously hanging on the teachers every word.

This slot was separated from that of the boy beside us by a lump of wood dividing the total area of the desk in half. In our case, unknown to me, this lump of wood was loose.

Even at six, Bert had a vicious streak in him that was amply veneered by that boyish, chummy, pally, demeanour for which he was well known. In fact, I would be doubtful that there is more than a dozen people who have been privy to his 17th face, the one that puts Pol Pot and Idi Amin into the Mother Therese league. These few people have witnessed levels of sadism completely at odds with the gamboling friendly Irishman Bert usually portrays.

And he delivered it all with a simple, charming, disarmingly impish grin, completely bereft of malice or forethought. He would offer you a sweet and poke your eye out using the very same set of facial muscles, the same friendly grin.

After sitting with him for a few months at school people could not understand why I didn't play with him in the yard or hang around with him in the street at home. Nobody associated my bout of bed wetting or frequent nightmares with the delightful little boy I sat beside at school.

And I made sure nobody, especially Bert, noticed that I was standing at the far side of the room to him when we were allocated our seats the following year. When poor Fred Wilson was presented with the privilege I felt a wave of elation, scarcely matched by the pity I felt for that poor lamb ambling up to the slaughter.

Fred Wilson still has the stutter he developed that following year, and when he gets tired he has a nervous twitch that starts in his left eye, works its way down his face, and ends the routine with a curl of his lip. I met him shortly after the leaving certificate and he had a job in the bank. How he got it I do not know because he was the shiftiest looking character I'd met in a long time, constantly looking sideways and jumping away from you. It probably had no connection.... I'm sure.

What can you do with a lump of wood?

I'll tell you what you can do with a lump of wood….
What a six-year-old DID with a lump of wood, not
six by eighteen inches long. I used think he sat up
nights dreaming new tricks he could play with that
piece of wood.

The first trick came before I was even aware there
was a piece of wood there at all.

The first I realised there might be something amiss
was when I came in one morning to find I couldn't fit
my school bag into the slot under my desk. It had fit
the day before and I spent a good five minutes
pushing and poking the leather bag into a hole into
which it just would not fit. Bert just sat there
watching me with a bemused look on his face.

"What's the matter Ben?" he innocently asked me as I
got more and more frustrated. I explained my
dilemma and he considered the possibilities. After a
few minutes he had me convinced that my bag had
expanded due to the rainy weather outside. I took a
lot of convincing, but eventually succumbed to the
notion and agreed to shove my bag in sideways
instead of lengthways.

I sat for a week with that bag sticking into my
stomach until someone noticed and asked me why I
was putting my bag in that way. I explained that my
bag had grown due to the wet weather and wouldn't
fit the other way any more. He looked at me as if I
had lost my marbles. Who in their right mind would
think that school bags grew if you watered them?
Was I an idiot or what?

"Let me try," he said, grabbing my bag from under the desk and rotating it to put it into the slot properly. It fit and I had no idea how it had come about. I went back to putting the bag in the correct way for a few days and then again one day I came in and it wouldn't fit. I was quite beside myself at this stage, mainly because it hadn't been raining and the growth theory wouldn't compute any more.

This time, however, I wasn't giving up and tried shoving and wedging with a fervour greater than the previous time. When trying to wedge it in from an angle I felt the middle block of wood shift. I stopped, thinking I was damaging the desk, and had a closer look. There was a wedge of paper holding the block where it was. The wedge was far enough into the desk on Bert's side so that I wouldn't notice it from my side.

Realisation dawned. He had been inching the block over to make my side smaller and his larger, and had secured it with last week's test paper. I was furious and when I launched into him when he came in he laughed and said it was just a joke, had I no sense of humour.

The secret was out then though, and we both knew we had a special desk. It became a game between us, shifting the block over and back under the desk. As we played, different games emerged and one day he suggested I stick my hand inside to the back of the desk behind the block and wave at him around the block so that he could see me waving from his side.

Like and eejit I did this and once I had my hand in position he rammed the block against the back of the desk and effectively locked my hand into the back of the desk.

He smiled at me as I realised what he had done and ignored my pleas to be released. The time for the teacher to arrive into the classroom was fast approaching and to be caught in this position would have been to attract a large dose of punishment, and the ritual humiliation that went with it.

Close to tears I begged him to let me go but with that same smile he looked at me, enjoying my pain, frustration, humiliation, fear and rising anger. We both heard the teacher's footsteps in the hall and my mind raced as they turned into the door of the classroom. As the classroom hushed to silence and discovery was imminent, he gave the block a final thump and let go the hold he had on it. I straightened up in the desk and, with eyes watering, busied myself with my books for the class.

We didn't speak for days, but it wasn't long before his natural friendliness and a fervent apology won me over again.

Then came the pivot. The pivot was another clever trick Bert devised.

Half way along the block he stuck a tack in both the top and bottom edges of the plank. Then he wedged the plank back in place. With the tacks acting as pivot points, the block rotated on the halfway point. Bert would swing the near side of the plank towards himself, meaning the far side swung through my half of the desk, sweeping whatever was under my desk onto the floor.

He could only do this on days that I didn't have my school bag, which was seldom enough, so he had a few test runs that I'd soon forget before he delivered his particular piece of malice. The test runs were performed before school, when he would gleefully tug the plank and sweep my lunch or pencils or whatever onto the floor. He would sit with that chummy smile as I scrabbled around on the floor to collect my stuff before the teacher came in.

During the marbles season I had a scunger and three marbles in under my desk. The scunger was a glorious piece of metal, which I had rubbed to a serious state of shininess. It was the envy of the class, not least to my 'best pal' Bert. Like an eejit I held it under the desk and while Mrs. McGuinness was delivering her explanation of the mysteries of four times tables Bert grabbed the plank and swept the collection of marbling delights out from under the desk.

The racket was enormous. First the scunger hopped off my lap and onto the floor, making a loud banging sound followed by the constant rolling rumble as it made its way across the wooden flooring. Just as the class was getting over the horror of the scunger, the three marbles, that I had been trying to keep from falling from my lap in a panicked scrabble to catch them, dropped one by one onto the floor and struck a lighter but equally horrific melody across the floorboards.

I nearly died on the spot. Mrs. McGuinness went ballistic. Not a woman for holding her temper at the very best of times, she erupted with a passion at this interruption to her teaching.

I was hauled unceremoniously by the ear up to the top of the class. At this stage I was incoherent with fear and shock. Tears flooded down my face obscuring the sight of thirty other boys trembling in the presence of such rage.

I was totally incapable of denying the charges of 'playing with marbles in MYYYYYY Classroom', and while any pleading or denials would have been a complete waste of time, the truth could never have been told. Imagine ratting on somebody else in the class…. Bert would never do such a thing…. What a story to dream up just to get out of trouble.

I was in the soup, and it was scalding.

Five strokes (more like lashes) of the cane, one for each marble and two for the scunger, were delivered along with a stinging stream of verbal abuse. I was mortified and sobbed for the rest of the morning. The scunger and marbles were confiscated, never to be seen again, and Bert tried to wangle out of it by saying his arm slipped.

Like hell it did.

His final trick was the strap of school bag getting caught at the back of the wood. When I pulled out my bag at the end of day the wood came out with it. The plank of wood slammed noisily against the seat of the desk and even more loudly onto the floor.

What a pantomime the teacher made of this piece of mindless vandalism. There I was, wrecking the school furniture, dismantling the very fibre of the school, willfully destroying the school property. She threw the book at me and then proceeded to give me six of the best in front of the whole class, as an example of what happens to little boys who step out of line. I was distraught, and dear Bert was The Innocent, scarred by the fracas, eager to please the teacher and overtly mindful of his seat companion.

The Janitor nailed the plank of wood firmly in place after that, but Bert had other tools to employ in an endless string of sadism doled out over that long year.

I think he had begun to tire of inflicting pain and humiliation on me by the end of that year. I was becoming inured to it and my reactions were not as satisfying for him as they had been previously. He had other fish to fry and poor Fred Wilson was next on the pan.

Not that Fred was the only one in the entire world to suffer. Although I have no proof, I suspect the other people intimately close to Bert endured the same onslaught of malicious trickery.

His mother was an alcoholic, and while that proves nothing, it does leave one wonder. His sister died at a young age, and while we were never told how exactly she died, there was a rumour that she had commit suicide.

As the years went on I had cause to meet up with Bert on occasion, but the outcome was always the same, and I was never encouraged to change my impression of him. I always left with a stinging sense of having been taken for a ride and knowing beyond any shadow of a doubt that I never wanted to set eyes on this guy again.

When I was 17 I was going out with this girl called Frieda. Now Frieda was a beautiful girl, with blonde hair, catching blue eyes, the most heart-stopping smile and a nice body to boot. She was about three inches shorter than me, which made her quite small, since I was only about five foot nine.

Overall, she was a picture of petite vulnerability that brought out a man's (or boy's) desire to protect, possess and defend. We were in love and had been tipping away for about three or four months. It may not seem long now, but when you're 17, three months is wedding ring material.

She lived across the town from me and we used meet up after school every day. Then on a Friday night we'd go together to the local hop. Her family knew my family and my family knew hers. It was all very homey and happy and, in the nicest sense of the word, innocent.

While both of us knew the facts of life (in explicit detail according to our own minds) and had indulged in what we would have termed 'heavy petting' more than the once, we had never engaged in 'full penetrative sex', a term we only learned years later. We knew what it was, all right, but didn't feel either of us were ready for this large step, and were both quite happy to take our time on that one.

We had discussed it in detail, as we discussed everything, and had concluded that it was well worth waiting for. What we were doing at the time was quite enough to be going on with. There were things Frieda could do to me that would have me quivering for a week and things I had done to Frieda that left her smiling for quite a while afterwards. There was plenty more to come that left 'the real Mac Coy' a none too urgent requirement.

From time to time I'd see Bert at the local hop of a Friday night. For loads of reasons I'd avoid him like the plague. Despite talking about everything to Frieda, I never went into too much detail about Bert. For one thing, we rarely met him so there was no reason to raise a bad story where there was none needed. And for another thing I did not want her to have anything to do with him. She didn't need the likes of him in her life and I was fiercely protective of her.

It happened one Friday that we bumped into Bert almost immediately we entered the school hall. The place was fairly empty so it was hard to avoid him and I was forced by the situation to introduce Frieda to Bert, Bert to Frieda. He smiled his perfectly formed set of teeth at her, and flashed his puppy dog brown eyes down at her from his towering six feet. All man and charm he exuded sex and confidence. He ran his fingers through his lush black shoulder length hair, curling the sides behind his ears with both hands at the same time, his elbows raised to show off his pecs. He was politeness itself, as would be expected, but underneath I could sense something else in Bert. In the very deepest pit of my stomach I shuddered and felt not just a little queasy. As soon as I could I steered Frieda away and got us involved in deep conversation at the far side of the room.

Two or three times during the night I caught Bert trying to make inroads into our air-space or conversation, but I was able to side step the approach and avoid the encounter without making it obvious to Frieda.

She was a little curious about Bert though, and made a point of asking how I knew him. I was very dismissive, saying I had been in the same class as him at school, but didn't encourage the conversation. I went so far as to say "You don't really want to know him." which, in hindsight, might not have been the best thing to say. It only peaked Frieda's curiosity.

It was about a week or two later that Frieda began to have 'a lot to do' after school. At first it didn't seem all that strange. We were both coming up to our mock Leaving Certificate and had a good bit of extra studying to do. But after a short while she wanted me to stop meeting her after school, saying that she had extra study sessions after school and would go home with the other girls from the class. I didn't disbelieve her, I had absolutely no reason why I should, but it worried me a little.

Then on the Friday night she didn't want to go to the hop. She had too much work to do. She even suggested I go on alone.

It felt strange to be at the hop on my own. I hadn't been to it without Frieda for months. There were all the usual people there and I had a good night chatting to all my friends.

And also to Frieda's friends who, strangely enough, didn't have so much work that they couldn't go to the hop. I figured it was my imagination that they were looking at me strangely, that it was just that I was alone and they were used to seeing me with Frieda.

I left early, and decided on a whim, to take a slight detour past Frieda's house. I really didn't know why I went that way. I didn't intend on dropping in to her. It was, after all, nearly one in the morning. I just wanted to be near her and walking past her house was the nearest I could get just at the moment.

I was walking up the road towards her house when I noticed someone standing outside. Curious, I squinted into the distance. No, it wasn't one person, it was two people… and they were VERY close together.

Embarrassed I walked a little slower, in case I was interrupting a couple stopping on the way home for a bit of passion. It was only when I was a few yards away that I realised I knew them both. Frieda had her back to the gate and Bert had his back to me.

I was gobsmacked. I didn't know what to do. I had almost stopped at this stage and must have made some sound because Frieda opened her eyes and let out a start of amazement and pushed Bert away from her.

The three of us faced each other in the street and I looked from one to the other of them. Words were spoken by all of us all at once.

"Why? How?"

"Ben, I'm so sorry…"

"Ah, Ben, how are you? What has you this end of the town at this time of night?"

Suddenly Frieda opened the gate and ran into her house. We both looked after her as she ran up the path, fumbled at the door and eventually slammed it shut behind her.

I looked at Bert and he looked at me. I should have known. He had on him that same look of complete innocence. He smiled.

"Nice girl," he said, and went to walk down the road with me.

"You shithead," I said, and walked in the opposite direction, back the way I had come.

I tried phoning Frieda the following day, but her mother said she was not well and was asleep in bed. On Sunday it was the same, but I met some of her friends after Mass and asked them what was the story. Eventually Betty, walking back towards home with me, confided that Frieda had been seeing Bert once or twice over the past fortnight.

I was devastated, to say the least, and didn't function too well over the following weeks. I dug myself into my books, if I remember rightly, and only went out of the house to go to school.

When I did see Frieda, it was as if she was always in the distance and moving away from me… in a hurry. We didn't speak again before the Mock Leaving Certificate exams and it was a week before the actual examinations, nearly two months later, that I got to speak to her again.

She was a changed person… and we had very little to say to each other. Somehow she seemed sadder and not as bubbly. It was as if she had lost something very important. It was funny, because although I knew she wasn't still seeing Bert, we never mentioned him.

Bert left for England immediately after the exams, and Frieda had her baby shortly after Christmas. Ironically, I was the Godfather, but I could never look at Frieda again the same way. We were great friends, and still are, but whatever it was we had that was special was gone. Gone forever.

I cursed Bert McBride that time and every moment since.

Chapter 2

So when I looked up at him again from my pint it as with an effort of will that I did not throw it over him. Maybe I should have and that would have been the end of it. But I didn't. I took another sup out of my pint and listened to him ramble on about how he had been over in London and just come back a couple of months ago.

He was still the tall handsome man about town, with thick black hair and sad brown eyes that went a long way to melting a lady's heart. He looked strong and confident, but somehow had that disarming vulnerable air to him which made him less intimidating and more endearing.

It took him quite a while to finish his story and I was sufficiently hungover and letting the hair of the dog have its effect on my bruised and battered innards that I just let him take the floor.

He had been over in London before, he said, but this time it was different. This time he had got himself a brilliant job in a computer company writing software. He had been dealing with big insurance companies and they had wonderful canteens, and loads of beautiful women. The way he went on about the women you'd think we didn't have any in Dublin, that they were all living in the Insurance Companies in London. But I didn't say anything. I just supped another swig out of my pint and nodded.

Behind his head I could see the sunlight out on the Rathmines Road and hear the distant muffled sounds of the traffic. I could smell the musty Saturday afternoon smell of the pub in my nostrils and I left it all drift over me. I'm sure the pub smells like that any early afternoon after the doors open and the air begins to sweep in though the seats, blowing out last night's smoke and not quite managing to take the smell of drink with it. I breathed it in healthily and slowly turned my attention back to the bollix.

"She was a beautiful lass. Just like our Frieda..." he was saying. "She came from Galway but she'd been living in London for a few years and she took me under her wing."

It was a second before I registered what he'd said, but I could see he noted my reaction without skipping a beat in his story. My heart began to thump uncontrollably and my brain went into an absolute swirl wind of neutral.

"She lived over the other side of London, in Croydon, but she used to spend a lot more time in Camden than she did there. The crack was better and sure... wasn't I there as well." he laughed.

Not quite knowing what I was doing I put my glass down and forced a smile, mumbling something about going to the loo.

"Not feeling the best after last night, eh?" he shouted after me as I made my way across the half empty pub to the men's room.

I snarled at my reflection when I went inside. My insides hadn't woken up yet so I didn't need to go anywhere near the urinal. I just grabbed the side of the sink and swayed back and forth for a few minutes. Another snarl at my reflection.

"Finish your pint and politely make your exit," I told myself into the mirror. "Simple as that."

I nodded sagely, and I nodded back at me. Between us we found the courage to push myself off the washbasin and salute each other good-bye. With a wink we bolstered up our confidence. "Finish your pint and we're off."

It seemed darker in the pub when I went back out and when I parked my bum back on the seat opposite him he was all solicitous and concern.

"Are you feeling all right mate?" he asked as he put a friendly hand on my shoulder. "One too many last night. Don't I know the feeling well. And me whittering on like nothing else. I should have more consideration."

I saw my opening. Here I could wander into this concern and make my exits, pleading a need to be alone and nurse my hangover. My meat and my manners.

"Indeed," I laughed with an air of world weariness. "The morning after the night before...."

I was just about to say "I'd better be off soon..." and shuffle off the seat, when he beat me to the post.

"Another pint is your only man."

He couldn't have choreographed it better. Just as he was saying it the barman came up behind me and placed two fresh pints on the bar in front of us.

"Thanks mate. What's the damage?"

He'd obviously ordered them while I was in the bog. I looked at the pints and at him, paying the barman and making small talk over the difference between the price of a pint here and in London. He even effected a London accent for the whole of the conversation and only dropped it when the barman had moved on down to the other end of the bar.

I couldn't crank up a reaction. I was still numb.

I shrugged. Maybe that was the safer way to be. Maybe I should sink into the ignoramus, drunken, hungover thicko role and nod my way through the second pint. It wouldn't be too difficult. Bert had launched into a story about the price of drink in London, and how himself and Louise used drink like royalty in Camden Town most every other night. What a wonderful place it was and what glorious times they had.

Then suddenly his mood changed, and he looked at me straight in the face. It was the look that said 'I'm opening my heart to you here and it's only my closest friends would hear such a confidence.' The 'you should be honoured' wasn't exactly obvious in the look, but it was implied.

"But then it all changed, Ben."

The genuine feeling of empathy was squeezed from my unwary soul. I looked back with a mild concern welling up inside me.

"For no apparent reason she just up and left me." With a look of anguished disbelief on his face he looked deep into his pint. I was almost tempted to reach over and lay a friendly hand on his shoulder to comfort him in this troubled time of his. It was only my natural reserve that staunched such a display of affection in a public house on a Saturday morning.

"There one day and gone the next." He took one last look at the small amount of Guinness in the bottom of the glass, put the glass to his mouth and downed it in one. With a sense of distracted contemplation, he placed the glass a few inches behind the one the barman had just left, sighed and with that same air of introspection, he fingered the moisture on the outside of the fresh pint, and shrugged.

"Life," he declared, "is not always easy."

Again he looked at me with that mournful look. I avoided his eyes and finished my own pint. Picking up the fresh glass I saluted him and, with a flourish I did not feel, said "onwards and upwards", taking a first sip from the creamy head.

As if shrugging off a cloak of great weight, he threw his shoulders back and picked up his glass.

"Onwards and upwards," he saluted, clinking my glass off his, and swigged a mouthful.

"Time for the little man," he said, slipping off the stool. "I'll be back momentarily."

I pondered my pint, held in my two hands between my knees in front of me. My shoulders sagged and I felt morose in the extreme.

"I could just leave," I thought. "Just up and walk out the door." I looked at the door, as if judging the distance. But I knew I wasn't doing anything of the sort. I had no intention of moving anywhere in a hurry. In an instant I had an image of Bert racing down the Rathmines Road with that pained look on his face, saying at the top of his voice "Why did you leave? Did I say something wrong? Are you all right?" I couldn't face the prospect. I was almost relieved when he returned. I would just have to wait until he let me go.

"Busy enough in here, for a Saturday afternoon." he said as he sat back up on the stool beside me. We looked around the half light of the pub at the dozen or so groups of people having their drinks and chatting in friendly relaxation. There were quite a few who were obviously out shopping for the day and taking time out for a gentle pint. There were others who had come in to read the days papers and were minding nobody's business but their own. A couple at the end of the bar were in the first throes of love and had eyes only for each other and beside them three lads were knocking great crack out of some football match that had happened the night before. All in all a comfortable place to be.

"Aye, busy enough," I replied.

There was a silence between us for a moment. I was in a hurry to fill it, but could think of nothing nice to say. I could see that Bert was eyeing me out of the corner of his eye.

The first pint was beginning to sink into my bloodstream and the awakening was slowly happening. The lethargy of the morning was clearing away and, while I wasn't going to light any fires in the ensuing conversation, the moron was fading and I could sense that Bert was aware of this.

"Have you been down home recently" he asked, as if for no reason other than to make conversation. But I had a deeper feeling that there was something behind it.

"Not for a few weeks" I said. "Everything was fine. And you?" I looked at him and raised an eyebrow... the question.

"Not since I came back."

He paused.

"Not much reason any more."

"Indeed," I nodded sagely, giving great attention to the head of cream on my drink as I swirled the half pint in the glass.

Somehow he was nearly finished his pint and he swirled the mouthful left in the bottom of the glass and looked at it expectantly, and then at me.

The realisation that he had bought the first two pints was sickeningly obvious, and the implication of the looks gloriously unsubtle.

"Should we have another?" I asked rhetorically.

"We may as well," he said as I hailed the barman and motioned at the two empty glasses. The barman nodded back and began to fill two more pint glasses from the Guinness pump.

"Indeed... not much reason to go home these days," he mused as the pints appeared on the bar in front of us and I paid the man the money with a few polite grunts.

"Except Cathal."

I looked at him in total bewilderment. Who the fuck was Cathal?

"A lovely lad. Growing up to be quite an angel."

Still I had no idea who he was talking about. All his family had either died or left the town. There was nobody left there for him. What was he on about? Who was this Cathal?

I looked at him in growing confusion and he just mused away into his pint, as if he had a video production going on in there.

He looked up and saw my confusion.

He started, as if surprised that I was confused.

"Cathal," he said, as if repeating the word would jog my memory.

I moved my head back and forth to signal that nothing new had come to my attention. My eyes widened to express that I still hadn't a notion who he was on about.

"Cathal..." he said again, "Frieda's kid."

My face must have exploded in disbelief. I couldn't think of a word to say. My confusion must have been blatant.

"You didn't know?" he asked, as if this was the source of my confusion. "Surely you knew.

"No, no, you must have known.

"Sure everybody knew... It's such a small town....

"And everybody knew it was my child....

"Didn't they...."

He was rambling now. I could see he was ever so slightly lost as to what it was that was confusing me.

"I thought it was all about the place. Sure isn't that the reason I went to London. And that the reason I asked her to come with me.

"But she wouldn't. She had to have the baby and bring it home.

"Damn near killed my mother."

He was back into the video footage in the head of his pint. The injustice of it all was palpable in the musty air of the pub.

I was so incredulous I was struck dumb. He took this as encouragement and rambled on about how he had fled to an uncertain future in London. How he had cut himself off from 'everything Irish' for nearly two years as he laboured in one building site after another, filled with remorse and guilt.

He made himself sound like the prodigal son by the time he got to the part where he felt it was time to face up to it all and go home.

And then he did go home and was welcomed with open arms by a forgiving mother. He had found the strength within himself to meet Frieda again and be introduced to his own flesh and blood, Cathal. He had cried when he had taken the little bundle into his arms, and hugged him to his chest. Cathal had said "Da Da" and wrapped his arms around his neck.

I swear I could see a little moistening in his eyes as he recounted this pile of garbage to me that Saturday afternoon in Slatterys of the Rathmines Road. I remembered a totally different story told by Frieda's mother a month after it happened.

He signaled to the barman.

I went to the bog.

Arrogant as you please, he had marched into their garden on a Sunday afternoon.

"Where is my little son?" he had asked as if it had only been the previous Sunday he had been around last. Cathal was chasing the cat around the flower bed and was suddenly yanked into this strange man's arms. Startled and afraid he had burst into a terror-stricken howl and struggled furiously.

Undaunted, Bert had held the child at arm's length saying "Don't you know your own father? What sort of a child are you at all?"

At that the child went apoplectic and it was only by getting Bert out of the garden and away from the house did they get him to calm down again. Ever since, the child burst into tears and ran behind his mother, or grandmother, or anybody standing nearby, to get away from him any time he'd make an appearance.

But that's not a story to tell in a pub on a pleasant Saturday afternoon.

I washed my hands slowly in the washbasin and dried them methodically using the hopeless hot air contraption on the wall. By the time I got back outside a match had started on the TV and our attention was diverted. He put my mobile phone back on the bar, where I had left it earlier. It never even occurred to me to get annoyed with him for picking it up.

We drank our fourth and fifth pint watching the match. I ended up buying the last pint, purely out of a sense of guilt. Half way through it I admitted defeat, and in a slurred voice said I had to go.

"I was on my way to get my breakfast when I met you" I explained.

"Always the wuss," he countered, not at all happy that his toy was going home.

"Whatever," I shrugged, as I lurched off the stool and headed for the toilet.

I had only opened the door when the vomit rushed up from my stomach. I just about made it to the sink and threw up at least three pints of liquid. In an instant it was over and I felt relieved and sobered. I washed out the sink and then my mouth and looked at the vision in the mirror.

"Go home Ben," it said to me. "What more can he do?"

I washed my hands, dried them in my pants and gingerly opened the door.

He was watching the match commentary and nodding wisely at the broadcaster. "Just as drunk as I am," I thought, making a quick dash for the side door. Once outside I squinted at the sunlight and leant for a minute against the pub windowsill. Once I had caught myself I lurched into my standing and headed around the corner onto the Rathmines Road.

"And where do you think you're going?" he said, standing in the doorway of the pub. "I thought it was you, slinking like a criminal out the back door."

"I'm going home," I said. "I've to meet Marian at seven, and I can't be entirely drunk." It was a lie. I had no intentions of meeting Marian, or anybody else later on. But he wasn't to know that.

"Marian, is it? And who is this Marian, tell me?"

I looked at him and I was back in a hall in Limerford.
His face was a mask of innocence and he was all
politeness and charm. Every fibre of my being
wanted to tell him about this girl I was falling in love
with. He was willing me to open my heart and tell
him the intimacies of our relationship. I could feel
the force of his personality drawing the information
out of me.

"Oh, someone in work throwing a party," I lied. "A
bit of a flat warming. I said I'd give her a hand out
getting things ready"

"Must be quite a friend to go to all that trouble?" he
pushed. "Mind if I tag along?"

Suddenly I was defending a non-existent workmate
from a gatecrasher with more resolution than I ever
had for anything before. All that was going through
my mind was "I gotta get rid of this guy. I gotta lose
him."

"I gotta eat," I said. "I need something in my
stomach."

I headed down towards home before I realised I had
no food in the flat. As if reading my thoughts, he
suddenly threw his arm around my shoulder and
offered to cook.

"I have some stuff in my place" he said. "Let's go
back and cook something up. It'll be a gas."

Not for the first time that day he shepherded me down the street towards our destiny.

We arrived at the door of his flat as the darkness fell, and in the quiet of the evening I paused to reluctantly admire where he was living. It was a quiet off the beaten track sort of place with its own front door around the side of the house. As he fumbled for his keys I admired the neat little path around the side of the house, the sheltering bushes, and the complete privacy of the place.

"What a nice change this would be for me away from the nosey Mrs. Blake downstairs from my own flat." I thought.

"Nice place you have here," I remarked as he opened the door and made his way into the spacious living room cum kitchen.

The furniture was old, but not as old and uncoordinated as it was in my own flat. Here the furniture was all seventies, and the Formica kitchen unit all of the same type, if a little worn and used looking. He had a sofa in the middle of the room facing the TV and to the side of that, a wall of kitchen cabinets, sink, cooker and fridge. There was space and a sense of proportion, even if it was all a little dark, with brown cabinets and the walls and floor a dark magnolia creamy sort of colour.

"It's not so bad," he said, barely concealing the gloat in his voice. "Now, what do you fancy?"

He looked around the room as if figuring what food was in the place that we could cook up.

"There's some spuds in the bag there, if you'd like to peel them. I have some sausages in the fridge we could fry up."

He picked up a pair of Marigold rubber gloves and threw them in my direction. "Put them on you laddie, so as not to ruin your delicate hands"

I caught them mid-air and before I knew what I was doing I had them on and could feel the sticky damp feeling of dirty water inside them. I could see him watching me out of the corner of my eye for a reaction, but I wouldn't give it to him. He turned on the radio and the sound of a DJ interviewing some bloke from Cork came on.

"Where do you keep your knives?" I asked, as if buckling to the work. Truth be told, the prospect of bangers and mash was making my mouth water.

"In the drawer beside the sink, and you'll find a basin underneath to hold the skins."

I walked over to the sink unit and as I did the first chords of Hazel O'Connor and "Will You?" started playing on the Radio. I was struck cold and froze with my hand in the drawer.

This was Our Song.

Frieda and I used contort in a parody of anguished passion every time that came on in the local dance hall in Limerford. We'd twist and point and pretend we were sitting on a couch, passing tea to each other, all on the dance floor much to the amusement of our mates.

"God, that song brings me back," said Bert. "That Frieda wan. Boy but she was a goer."

It had come out by accident, and he didn't realise the impact it had, so he continued. "Gagging for it she was... would be tearing the pants off me, drooling at the mouth for it."

Suddenly I had the knife in my hand and it dug up against the material of his T-shirt.

"What did you say?"

He looked at me as if I was mad.

"You dirty scum bag," I exploded. "She was better than you were ever worth."

"Ease up man, she was only a slag. She was giving it to all the guys..."

Suddenly the knife was dug into his chest. With a mighty thrust I had pushed it up behind his rib cage. His eyes opened wide, and he stared at me in disbelief.

There was silence while both of us were locked in that same disbelief, and then the Sax played mournfully.

He clutched the knife in his chest and staggered backwards, trying to pull it out. But it was stuck... He couldn't move it. He stumbled backwards and bumped into the couch, falling back into it, ended up sitting as if he was watching TV with a knife in his stomach. The blood was dribbling down from his hands onto his khaki trousers.

The Sax stopped... and for a second there was complete silence in the flat. As if for an age we stared at each other, then the DJ came back.

"And that was Hazel O'Connor and 'Will You?'. Unforgettable... Requested there by Michael Murphy from Cobh in Co. Cork...." He continued on, but I was in another world.

He was sitting there in front of me, eyes wide open, staring at me. But I knew now he wasn't there any more. He was gone. The lights were on but there was nobody in. He couldn't do any more damage.

I felt as if the clouds had opened and the bright sunshine was streaming in on top of the two of us. But the room suddenly was too small for us. It was stifling and stuffy.

Boy George was on the Radio singing "Do you really want to hurt me?". I looked down at myself. I was still wearing those Marigolds, but there wasn't any blood on me.

Bert hadn't moved, and without going near him I knew he was dead.

I had killed him.

I turned out of the room and pulled the door behind me.

Without thinking I walked around the private pathway I had so admired only a half hour before hand and out the front gate. I walked up towards Ranelagh and three quarters down Mount Pleasant Avenue I saw a skip filled with household rubbish outside some house being renovated.

Only half thinking I tore off the Marigolds and threw them deep into the rubbish. Then I was out on the canal road and The Portobello pub was in front of me.

"A pint of Guinness" I said to the barman.

I looked around. The bar was packed.

I went to the loo and looked at myself in the mirror. Washing my hands I avoided my own eyes. My hands were stinking from those damn gloves. I washed them again with more soap.

The guy was just bringing up my pint when I arrived back at the bar. I paid for it and looked around. I knew nobody. The sporting results were on the TV.

I had another pint.

It was late in the evening when I staggered out of the Portobello and onto the bridge. I nearly got into a fight with a couple of lads heading into town, but they avoided me and left me to my own devices.

I don't remember getting home.

Chapter 3

I woke up the following morning and it was with a slow sense of unreality I realised what I had done.

Everything in the room was the same as the day before. The wardrobe door still hung open, strewn with most of my clothes airing for another wear. The pile of unwashed underwear and towels still sat in a mound on the floor between the wardrobe and the old veneer drawer unit. Each drawer was still half-open, exposing the contents to easy identification. The horrible flowery wallpaper still curled at every other split, and gaped openly beside the window, showing the damp yellow wall beneath. The room still had the same claustrophobic comfort of the womb with, I'm sure, an earthy animal odour. But there was something now very different in the room. It wasn't visible. It wasn't tangible. But with unerring certainty I began to absorb the fact that it was there. There was a murderer in the room.

All the horrible connotations that go along with that word were missing. There was no ogre. There was no slime. There was no dark dungeon eerie atmosphere. I was in my perfectly ordinary bedroom, looking at my perfectly ordinary curtains, in my perfectly ordinary bed. OK the bed hadn't had a change of sheets this month and might be considered to be a bit 'high', but that would be associated with a single lad living in a flat, as opposed to a murderer.

I tried to distinguish the defining characteristic that pulled me out as a murderer and I couldn't. It was an act in the past, a thought in my brain, an image that could only be recreated in my own imagination. No one else had seen or heard any of it. Had I imagined it all? Was it a wicked dream in the night that I could shrug off and forget about? Somehow I didn't believe it was.

The images flashed back in a frenzied succession of frightening clarity. The look on his face as I pushed in the knife. The blood oozing from his front. It was an eerie image, funny in an unreal and very unfunny sort of way. One hand grabbing the knife. The other hand trying to staunch the blood. The surprise in the eyes. The surprise draining to a vacant stare.

All images, but no longer the feeling of rage and cool determination. The overall feeling of justification. Now it was just pictures flying in and out of my mind.

The blood soaked shirt. The body sitting on the couch.

The sax playing in the background. Then the silence, and the vague sound of the traffic coming in the window.

These images were too real to be the memories from a dream in the night. It's funny that I call it a dream instead of a nightmare. And the images are 'real' instead of 'awful'. It is as if that now I have been there the situation is no longer frightening or horrific.

I've seen a pig being killed in the barn and the blood and guts that this job entails. As a child I looked at this and absorbed it as a fact.

Wow! Have I become so amoral as to parallel the taking of a human life with the killing of a pig? Would I now kill at random? Am I the archetypal murderer? Is the chubby little blonde girl in the shop on the corner my next target? Am I out of control?

I pulled the covers over my head, hoping to go back to sleep. To sleep perchance to dream... aye that's the rub. Those images flashed back at me.

I shot open my eyes and focussed on the ceiling, on the light shade, on the stippled paint, on the damp spot in the corner. Anything. Anything that was real and ordinary and everyday.

Suddenly the bed was no longer comfortable. I wanted to get out of it. I wanted to be up and about.

I threw back the covers and stood up in the room. I was naked. I saw myself in the mirror and I looked exactly the same as yesterday. Still the same messed brown hair, still five foot nine, and still the same blue grey eyes. Still the same looseness in the tummy - not fat, but needing a bit more exercise. Still the fuzz on my groin, with a respectable projection protruding. Still the same round cherubic, soft on the eye but not particularly handsome, face.

Was this the face of a murderer? No, no, it couldn't be. It's the same face as it was yesterday.

So was I a murderer yesterday…. I just hadn't got around to it yet.

If that was the case everything is explained and normality has resumed because it was never interrupted. I am the same as yesterday. The flat is the same as yesterday.

Or as much as it ever was in an ever-changing world. A little more hair on the chin. I rubbed it to check. To check what? I knew I wouldn't shave today. It was Sunday and I never shave on a Sunday. Ever since I was a boy I never shaved on a Sunday. The only reason you would shave on a Sunday was for Mass, and I stopped that long before my face took up producing hair.

Ah! Normality resumes. I'm having intellectual conversations with myself again. I pulled on a pair of jocks and trousers and went into the kitchen and put on the kettle. By the time it had boiled and I had watched a few minutes of the TV I had almost parked the murderer bit.

But when I was taking the spoon out of the drawer to make the tea I saw the knives and the sense of the knife digging into his body just popped into my head. Like a visit from Great Aunt Dinah who used just appear on the doorstep with no warning whatsoever and stay for a week. Life would be unbearable for the week, but it would be so sweet after she left.

My mother would always say that it made you appreciate what you had to have a visit from Aunt Dinah. The peace afterwards was supreme.

I snapped shut the cutlery drawer and spooned the sugar into the cup.

The Spice Girls were on the television and I read the subtitled information panning across the bottom of the screen. Did you know that Geri Halliwell had a Spanish mother? Well, there y'are now. The things you learn on a Sunday morning.

I went over to the window and looked out on the street. It was a nice day. The sun was shining and there were a few fluffy white clouds in a perfectly blue sky. The trees cast clear shadows onto the pavement and I could smell the fresh clean Sunday air coming in the window. It was a Sunday you would want to be out in. I thought about a walk along the canal, or a walk into Stephens Green.

The street was empty of people and the cars were parked bumper to bumper along the side of the road. There was nobody moving very fast this Sunday morning.

A little breakfast and down to the Green.

The canal is a beautiful place on a Sunday morning. Walking along Grand Parade, with the ducks paddling in among the reeds and the swans gliding slowly in the water. The crisp clean air and the trees changing into their winter gear, the leaves yellowing and forming bundles of kicking material on the pathway.

None of the usual weekday traffic jams and none of the eerie solitude of the night-time. Sunday morning has an openness all of its own with a faint promise of a good clean future.

I sauntered across Leeson Street and along Mespil Road, keeping a perverse eye out for condoms left behind by the hookers who might have done business the night before. As always, I admired the big buildings along the road, solid houses still looking as if people might live in them. Past Paddy Kavanagh where he sits in all weathers, bronzed for eternity, and over Baggot Street to pick up a paper before I wandered around to Haddington Road for a hearty breakfast.

But for some reason the place was closed so I retraced my steps up Mespil Road and took my place in the Queue in Cafe Java. Marian likes that place and since I usually go there with her, I missed her not being there this morning. She had gone home to her parents on Friday evening and would be back later that evening.

Too late I remembered that I needn't have bought a newspaper. They usually have loads lying in the waiting seat in the window. Huh! More money than sense.

I was placed in a seat along the corridor and was soon digging into bacon and eggs, orange juice, toast and tea with a newspaper propped up in the teapot in front of me.

"Crime Rate Up" read the headlines. The article went through the list of mentionable crimes, including car theft, muggings, rape, burglary and murders. Each had percentage increases attached to them.
I wondered if my contribution yesterday would skew the statistics.

Suddenly I had a vision of Bert sitting on his couch, cold in a cold room, with the knife sticking out of his gut. The fork stopped mid way to my mouth and my heart lurched.

He was dead. I killed him.

I returned the fork to the plate and stared out into Leeson Street. I must have been staring into space for a while because one of the waitresses tapped me on the shoulder and asked me was everything all right.

"Oh. Sure. Sure. Fine." I snapped back to the present and nodded graciously at the lady. "I was miles away," I needlessly explained. "It's fine, fine." I assured her, and as if to prove the point I picked up the fork again and put the egg and toast into my mouth.

I was hungry so I finished off the meal and picked up the paper to leave. I went to the cash desk, paid for the meal and headed for the door.

Just as I reached the door a hand clasped me on the shoulder and I turned around to an accusing face. "You shouldn't have done that," said this tall bloke with an air of pompous authority.

With a gut wrenching feeling of being caught I nearly collapsed on the spot. How did he know? Did he live near Bert? Had he already been to the flat? Had he seen me enter... or leave?

I looked at him in absolute horror, guilt written all over my face.

"Wha????" I stammered.

"The paper," he said. "You shouldn't be taking it with you."

At this stage we had an audience. Several people had turned to look.

"What seems to be the problem?" The lady who served me was suddenly standing beside us.

"He's trying to nick the paper," said the big guy.

"I...." I stammered, obviously upset.

"He brought it in with him," said the waitress. "See, there is no cafe stamp on the front. He bought it himself."

I looked from the oaf to the waitress in complete confusion.

"I'm sorry sir, he obviously made a mistake," and turning to the idiot she sternly pointed to the waiting seat. "Maybe you'd like to sit down?"

He shrugged ignorantly and mooched to the seat and she turned to me again. I still was a little spaced. "I really am sorry sir, he was quite out of line." and seeing my spaced look continued, "Are you all right?"

"Yea, fine. Where is the loo?"

"Sure sir, out the door and up the stairs."

"Thanks." I turned and left, rushing up the stairs. I was hot and cold all at once and my stomach nearly delivered my breakfast onto the stairway but by the time I got to the loo I had swallowed it down again and was just out of breath, sweating profusely.

I sat down on the seat for a minute to regain my breath and slowly got back to normal.

By the time I unlocked the door and went to leave I was quite all right again. Outside the door was the waitress.

"Are you all right sir?" she asked. "You seemed to be quite upset with yer man."

I looked at her, bemused.

"He was a complete idiot. He must have had his eye on your paper. He was completely out of line. Are you all right?"

She was obviously worried and my staying in the loo for so long had obviously encouraged her concern.

I smiled at her, shrugging. "No. It's all right." I explained. "A bit of a hang-over. I was just taken a bit unawares. I'm not the full shilling this morning. But I'm all right. Thanks."

She seemed a little placated. "Are you sure. You took it a little badly. He was an ignorant sod. I was tempted to ask him to leave."

"No. No. I'm fine now. He was a bit of a bollix, but isn't the world full of them. It's people like you have to put up with them more than me. I'm fine thanks. Honestly."

I made to go down the stairs, then turned...

"Just rub it in while he's here," I grinned.

She laughed, enjoying it. "I will" she said. "I will."

"Take care." I said, "and thanks." We winked at each other, and I was out in the street.

The Leeson Lounge looked very tempting across the road but then I thought of Marian's reaction if I met her off the bus with a skinful on me, or worse if I failed to meet her at all.

"Home with you boy," I said. "It looks like it's going to rain anyway. Get home before it pisses out of the heavens on you"

I walked around by Leeson Park and wandered through Dartmouth Square.

"Ben, how are you?"

"Rachel. How are YOU? Long time no see. Are you living around here?"

"Yup. I'm sharing a flat here on the square. Moved in about a month ago. Two girls from where I work and myself. It's great. D'ye want to come in for a cup of tea? They're all away for the week-end and the place is dead quiet without them."

Before I knew it, she had me up the steps of the house and into this massive big kitchen.

"Isn't it just wonderful," she crooned as she put on the kettle and put the messages she had just bought into the presses and the fridge.

I wandered over to the window and looked out at the square. "What a fabulous view," I murmured, "you must be thrilled."

"Thrilled is not the word. I LOVE it here. And the girls are great. No rows... so far."

She rattled on and the conversation flowed. We had been at college with each other and had gone beyond the flirting stage. She was one of my many sisters and me one of her many brothers. We took up where we left off and brought each other up to date on events.

She was seeing a guy who was big in computers, drove a BMW and liked to eat out in fancy restaurants. He sounded like a right pratt, but I didn't need to say that. She was happy with him and who was I to point out my own little narrowmindednesses. She was delighted to hear about Marian and figured that since we now lived so close to each other we should all meet up for a jar sometime.

The afternoon passed easily and several mugs of tea later it began to grow dark outside and I looked at my watch. "Oh, shit. I'll be late. Marian's bus is in at seven and I want to drop into the flat before I go collect her. I better go."

"Is it that time already? Tom is due to call over shortly. Why don't you stay for a minute and meet him."

"I'd love to, honestly Rachel, but I must go. Let's get together for a jar before Christmas. Now that we know where we all are we can organise something."

We swapped numbers and I was out at the top of the big granite steps. Hugs and kisses and I went down the steps and onto the square. She waved me down the street and as I turned the corner I figured I saw a guy get out of a BMW and walk towards the house.

"That was close," I thought as I headed for home.

I just about made it to the bus as it pulled in along the Quays. Marian was thrilled to see me and me to see her. We hugged as if she'd been away for weeks instead of just the weekend.

She had her blond hair tied back in a ponytail and her petite face was tired from the travelling. As usual she had gone easy on the make-up and looked a good bit younger than her 23 years.

When I picked her up by the waist in a big hug it was almost as if I was lifting a child, so small and light she appeared, although in truth she's only about two inches shorter than me.

"C'mon, I need a pint after that bus ride. Let's go into Mulligans for a quick one before we go home."

So into Mulligans we went and found ourselves a spot just inside the door. While Marian stowed her bags under the table I went up to get the pints from the bar. By the time I came back she was settled nicely with a cigarette in her mouth and a gratifying smile on her face.

"So, what sort of week-end did you have without me?" she asked as a primer to telling me all about hers.

"Ah, quiet enough. I went out with the lads from work on Friday night and we ended up being the last to leave the pub. I was in a cruel state on Saturday. I stayed in bed for most of it and then went for a few pints in the Portobello. I had breakfast in Cafe Java this morning..."

"Ahhhh, without me...."

"And you never guess who I met on the way home from there."

A quizzical look.

"Rachel Fitzsimons from College. D'ye remember me telling you about her who's Da was a doctor in Athy and she thought a man without a car was not to be entertained."

We both laughed.

"Well, she's got a boyo with a BMW now and he sounds like a right wanker all together. She wants us to meet up for a pint before Christmas, but I'm sure we can avoid it somehow.

"How did your weekend go?"

"Ben, it was great. Me mother was in good mood. Me father had just won a few hundred quid in the pub draw on Friday night.... And better than all that Alan got himself a job.

"D'ye remember he was so depressed after the Leaving results and he didn't get enough for college? Well, it looked like he'd never find a job after that and after trying and trying just about everything he finally landed himself a job in the local garage. MickeyJoe in the Main Street said he'd take him on as an apprentice for a year and see how he works out. Isn't that great?"

"That's great altogether. And did he want to be a mechanic?"

"All his life. Ever since he was a child he's been tinkering around with bits and pieces. It's a job made for him. Mum is thrilled..."

"To have him out from under her feet...."

"...and Dad is thrilled...."

"To have him stop sponging on him..."

"So we went out on Saturday," she continued, studiously ignoring me, "to celebrate with a big lunch in the Grand Hotel, and spent the afternoon having the crack in the hotel bar. It was the best day ever."

"Ye must have had some heads on you this morning?"

"The house was a bit quiet this morning all right." she laughed, "but we were all up and about for dinner. And Mum had the whole fandango, roast lamb, marrowfat peas, cabbage, mashed potatoes, roast potatoes and lashings of gravy."

"Mmmmm. That sounds nice. Are you hungry now? I'd surely kill a Chinese now. I haven't eaten since breakfast."

"OK. Let's go. We'll get it up in Ranelagh and a bottle of wine to go."

And we were off.

****

It was Tuesday before I was really on my own again. Marian had her classes and was checking in on her own flat. I was sitting reading a book with the radio on.

I'd had something to eat and was settling in to a lazy night beside the fire. There was nothing on the TV that I wanted to watch so I had the book propped up in front of me and a mug of tea at my elbow.

I enjoyed these nights in on my own. The flat wasn't a palace, but it was my own. It wasn't always clean, but it was my own dirt too. There was just about room for the couch in the middle of the floor in front of the fireplace. Stretching your hand from one side of the couch you could touch the bedroom door, and at the other end of the couch you could open the drawers of the 'kitchen', a sink unit, fridge and a cooker covering the opposite wall. Behind the couch there was the dining table and it's two chairs beside the door to the hallway outside. The bathroom door was right next to the bedroom, which had been convenient on more than one occasion.

Flowery wallpaper was obviously the rage when the place was being decorated, although using the word decorated would probably be a slight exaggeration. None of the assembled pieces of furniture actually matched. The table and chairs were nineties Bargaintown. The kitchen was a mixture of thirties fridge, sixties cooker and home-made kitchen unit made by an amateur carpenter when four by one was the fashion. It had been larruped with paint so that the doors and drawers either stuck, or chipped off the layers of paint to show the raw wood beneath.

The couch was a comfortable spring-less collection of cushions covered in a red nylon stretch fabric with the occasional cigarette burn to give it character. Overall, the only thing that held the whole effect together was the comfortable smell of grime, fries, booze and take-aways that permeated the whole flat.

Tonight the smell was mainly fish and chips, with a little turf smoke from the peat briquettes on the fire burning in front of me.

I'll not say that Saturday afternoon hadn't crossed my mind over the past few days. It had. More than once... but not in any significant way that had me trembling in me boots. There were moments where I relived seconds, where something tapped on my spine and made me shiver for a split second. But I never had time to dwell on it, to really think about it.

Not like now.

Now it was me and IT, a book and a mug of tea. No need to say where the book came in the pecking order.

As if, on demand, I had a video going in my head.

But it wasn't a nasty.

There was the pub. The nice people in there on a Saturday morning.

The flat, and the nice quiet entrance to the place.

But then there was the Marigolds, and the power game...

And the ribbing...

And then he was saying it again...

"That Freida wan. Boy but she was a goer. Gagging for it she was... would be tearing the pants off me, drooling at the mouth for it."

It was all in slow motion. The leery grin on his face. The glint of lust in his eye. The creepy crawly cut of his gangly shoulders. Though I hadn't really noticed it on the day he was wearing a gold trinket around his neck. It was a Celtic cross. It seemed so obscene when you put his personality as a backdrop. It was almost like wearing swimming togs in a church. It wasn't wrong.... it just jarred.

Then the knife in my hand.

How did it get there? I don't even remember picking it up. Where did I get it?

Lucky it was such a sharp one. None of the ones in my kitchen drawer would have done any more than bruise him.

But suddenly it was in my hand and in his gut at the same time. It didn't seem to have taken much effort to push it in...

To so much effect.

He was dead in no time at all. He hadn't even time to
say anything...

Oh God. I never whispered the final Act of
Contrition in his ear.

Shit! He was off to hell anyway. I'd say they had a
good and comfy spot all ready and prepared for him.
My little act of contrition wasn't going to mess that up
on him.

That split second when it went into him. The sudden
lurch. The minuscule realisation that this was his
end. The wide-eyed look at me... The total silence...

The small falling back... him taking a hold of the
knife... holding it as if he was trying to pull it out...
but not having a hope of doing so. He was dead.
There was no energy in those hands. Just enough to
hold it... to take the flow of blood and carry it back
towards the couch...

The slow falling back into the couch and the open
eyes staring at me...

I saw it all and shivered there in front of the fire.

I had done it. I had killed him. It was me... and only
me. There was only the two of us there. I had killed
him. I was guilty.

Guilty.

But sorry?

Sorry! No. Not sorry. It had happened... just like slipping on a banana skin. I hadn't meant to do it... but now it was done I wasn't sorry.

Would I do it again?

No. I wouldn't do it again. I hadn't engineered it... hadn't meant for it to happen.

Had he been at the other side of the room...

Had I been opening the beans and had a tin opener in my hand the end would have been different. Maybe we would have fought, and damaged each other, and the flat, but I don't expect I would have killed him.

But the way it happened I was standing beside him picking up the knife when he said something stupid.

Hah. Stupid for him, but not unusual. That was HIM. It was how he talked, how he thought, how he did things.

The little bastard.

No. Sorry I was not.

But Guilty I was.

There was a dead body in Ranelagh and only I knew about it.

The tea was cold at my elbow but I had no more inclination to go around to his flat and check the body than I had to finish the mug of cold tea.

He was dead. He was gone. The world was shut of him. I was shut of him.

But still the video played.

Still the eyes stared at me from the couch.

I turned on the TV and watched the news.

No dead bodies found in Ranelagh.

I opened a can of Budweiser.

Shit. I killed him.

Chapter 4

It was the following week, and again in Cafe Java, that the news broke.

"Body found in Ranelagh" read the headline, a small one on page four.

"You're looking a bit better than you were last week," the waitress smiled at me.

"And feeling a lot better too," I replied.

Marian looked a bit quizzical at us.

"Some idiot was accusing your friend last week of pilfering the newspapers. Your poor man was dying of a hang-over and I had to step in and shut the eejit up."

"I hope you gave him hell," I asked, laughing.

"I sure did. By the time he was leaving he was so embarrassed I doubt he'll be back here in a hurry. Ignorant cretin, thought the world owed him homage. I had him believing you were going to sue us for harassment and if you did we'd have him in the courts alongside us. Before the end of the meal I had him give his name and address, witnessed by his girlfriend, who had to give her address as well."

Marian and I laughed at the joy of it.

"He even offered to pay for your next meal when you were in, but I didn't see him leaving any cash behind him.

"What'll you have this week?"

We made our orders and I filled Marian in on the details of the previous Sunday morning.

"What a cheek," said Marian. "Wouldn't you just love to give him one."

"I'm afraid all I wanted to do was die. I was mortified. At that stage I couldn't wait to just get out of here. Everybody was having a good gawk."

The orange juice and the tea came and we drifted into the papers.

> "The body of a young man was found
> dead in his apartment in Ranelagh. The
> discovery was made by the Landlords
> when they went to collect rent. The body
> is thought to have been in the flat for a
> number of days. The Gardaí are keeping
> an open mind as to the cause of the death,
> but at this point are following a specific
> line of enquiry."

"There's a place doing Yoga Classes in Rathmines."

"Ye Wha?"

"There's a place doing Yoga Classes in Rathmines."

"Oh, right. Are you interested?"

"Of course I am. Haven't we been talking about getting into a class for weeks now. And here is one in the paper. A starter class and then advanced classes later on."

The plates arrived with the bacon and eggs, the toast and the butters.

"Are you on?"

"Sure. What night is it on?"

"Wednesday nights. Seven to nine."

"Mmmm. That should be all right.

How much?"

"It doesn't say. It just gives a number. I'll give them a ring tomorrow and see."

"They're good classes."

The two of us looked up.

"They're good classes." repeated the waitress. "I started last year and it doesn't take long to get into it. It's very reasonable. I don't know what price it is this year but I remember last year I though it was great value for money."

"Excellent," I said as I rearranged the plates on the table and moved things around to allow the piles of food she was giving us fit on the small spaces available. "Are there many people in the classes?"

"Last year there were about twenty-five in the class. I think they restrict it to somewhere between twenty and thirty because a friend of mine was too late and was told to wait until the next time. So there must be some limit."

"And what sort of people are there?" asked Marian as I started buttering some toast.

The two ladies chatted on while I poured tea and my eyes wandered back to the newspaper propped up against the wall.

> "The dead man was in his twenties and his identity is not being released until his next of kin have been informed. It is understood that he was not a native of Dublin and had spent many years in England."

Suddenly I had a punch in the shoulder.

"Louise is going to meet us next Wednesday to show us around the Yoga place."

"Louise?"

Marian pointed, exasperated, at the retreating figure of the waitress.

"Louise. We were just talking to her. About the Yoga. Are you with us at all? What planet ARE you on? We were just talking about it. Will you put away that paper and not be so ignorant."

"Shades of my mother," I thought. "Sorry Luv. Sunday mornings," I said, as if that was to explain everything.

It was a pleasant breakfast with Louise dropping by from time to time to refill the coffees and chat a bit more. Then it was down town for a wander around the shops in the Stephens Green Shopping Centre and a stroll down Grafton Street.

****

The following week was surprising light on reports of the 'Dead Body in Ranelagh' as it became known.

I bought just about every paper that was published in Dublin. Once I had read through them I made sure to throw them away. The last thing I needed was for Marian to ask why I had suddenly taken to buying so many papers.

I can just imagine her standing in the middle of the floor in the flat with her hands on her hips. "What's this? You bought shares in the newspaper industry?"

No. Once I'd scanned the papers for stories about Bert I threw them away. I didn't even collect the articles. I wanted nothing to do with them. I only wanted to read what was written and be informed... to be ahead of the posse as you might say.

Marian wouldn't be long in putting two and two together if she came across a shoebox full of articles on a particular murder. She might make seven or eight instead of four, but she'd come to a conclusion that'd eventually lead to too many delicate questions that'd surely lead her to the big "Was it you did it?"

Monday had nothing. Neither had Tuesday or Wednesday. Thursday had a small piece in the Evening Herald where it was mentioned in an article about the crime rate that in the past month there had been so many muggings, such a many rapes, and a murder of a young man in Ranelagh. But nothing substantial in it to warrant comment.

On Saturday there was a big article on it in the Irish Times. It was one of these researched pieces that seemed to go through the whole thing. It wasn't very long. It mentioned the flat in Ranelagh, the fact that it was a young man in his twenties, the fact that he had been stabbed (It didn't even mention where.), the fact that no motive for the attack could be determined.

> "The apartment in which the dead man
> was found had not been tampered with in
> any way, which would lead Gardaí to
> assume the motive was not burglary.

While the circumstances of the death
would be considered suspicious, the
Gardaí are keeping an open mind as to the
cause of death.

Until his next of kin have been contacted
the Gardaí will not release the name of the
dead man. There is much speculation as
to his identity, but it is known that the
dead man is not from Dublin and spent
some time in England."

All in all, it was not the most enlightening of articles,
but it did lead me to assume they were not out hot on
the scent of the killer. It even hinted at suicide, which
gave me a glimmer of hope that they'd call off the
hunt at some stage.

Chapter 5

Did I go to the Funeral? Are you mad? I didn't even know he was dead.

Despite the fact that I must have read every word that was ever written on the subject of the murder, and seen every news report (every edition) that was ever broadcast, nobody had ever mentioned the fact that Bart McBride had been slain in his own living-room by a knife wielding psychopath. I had never been in a conversation, nor even overheard a conversation that mentioned his name.

Sure, in work and the odd time in the pub there was mention of that guy in Ranelagh who was stabbed, but only in passing and never more detailed than that.

So when the funeral came up I figured it would be inappropriate for me to go. In other words, questions would be asked about how I heard, and I would have been placed in a situation where I had to lie through my teeth from the moment I walked in the church to the moment I left the pub after the graveyard.

As it was, the only time it ever came up was in a very oblique way when somebody mentioned the guy who was killed in his flat in Ranelagh. Never a mention of a name, and no need to spin a story, tell any lies or conjure up a smoke screen. Best all round if I just didn't turn up. Turning up would have been to walk into the arms of the cops.

I can't imagine how it went. Most of his family is gone out of the town. His mother and father are dead and I've no idea where his brother got to. He might have a few uncles or aunts about the place, but finding them could be a bit of a performance.

So gathering a group of mourners could be a bit of a difficulty. I expect there'd be the usual morning churchgoers, my own Mother among them, who might fill out the church a bit. But I'd say the graveyard would be a pretty sparse event.

Yup. It would have been a bit outstanding if I had of turned up for that.

I can imagine it.

"And when was the last time you met him, Ben? Did you keep in touch with him a lot?"

"I didn't know you were particularly friendly with Bert. Were you good friends? Isn't it very good of you to come all this way to be here."

They'd be the leading questions. As the conversation would go on they'd have me out on the rack, teasing out the gory details of our meetings and hitting pay dirt when it came to the final interaction.

No. No. That was a funeral to be avoided.

****

There were a few articles in the papers the day after the funeral. The largest was about five paragraphs.

> "The funeral was held yesterday in Limerford of the young man found dead in his apartment in Ranelagh. He was Bert McBride (23) who had grown up in Limerford and moved to London shortly after his Leaving Certificate.
>
> Having worked for some years there, on building sites and in the computer industry, he returned to Ireland at the beginning of the year to seek employment in the burgeoning IT industry here.
>
> The funeral was attended by his relations and friends from the town of Limerford. The body is interred in the graveyard of the Church of St. Mordecai.
>
> His body was found a month ago, stabbed in the stomach with a carving knife. The reason for his death has still not been established.
>
> The police are keeping an open mind on the case and it is expected a decision will be made before the inquest which is due to be held in a month's time."

The other papers had even less in them, though I rooted through every one I could find. Even the Meath Chronicle only had a small piece in it.

> "Bert McBride (23) the young man found dead in his flat in Dublin, was buried last Tuesday in the graveyard of the Church of St. Mordecai, Limerford.
>
> The funeral was attended by relatives and friends who travelled from afar to pay their respects"

Never speak ill of the dead. I guess they weren't going to embarrass the relations any more than they had to.

Chapter 6

He was about three weeks buried and the whole thing seemed to have been pretty much swept under the carpet. I hadn't heard much about the whole thing in ages, but then again I'd been busy in work and keeping a low social profile due to lack of funds.

Marian was all wound up about a house party her friend was having in Ranelagh. Some friend of hers from school had just moved into a new flat and they were having a house warming. It was billed as a pretty wild event for several reasons. Firstly, there were three of them in the flat and friends from all three were coming together in the one party. Secondly, the place was a complete floor of an old house and, by all accounts, enormous. Finally, the stories going around about Marian's school buddy had to be seen to be believed, and since I hadn't seen any of it I was impressively sceptical. If a fraction of the stories were true, this woman was amazing and any party she'd grace with her presence would suddenly catapult into the social event calendar.

I was 'merely tagging along', and because I was up to my goolies in work, had given the whole thing little thought other than looking forward to a bit of crack and a lot of pints on Saturday night. Marian was organising and arranging, I was attending. All I needed to know was the level of formality of what I would wear (old jeans or new jeans) and how much drink we should buy beforehand.

Everyone was meeting in McSorleys and it would all happen from there.

At seven o'clock Marian arrived full of bustle and excitement. She had on her new red dress and she looked wonderful. I, of course, was still lying on the couch watching the TV. After she had done a twirl, given me a hug and a kiss, she was off into the kitchen (sic!) to make a cup of coffee.

"Get up off that couch, you lazy cabbage" she shouted over at me, "and get yourself into the bathroom. We have to be in the pub at half past eight."

"Half past eight," I groaned, "I'll be plastered by eleven."

She laughed as she put the coffee into the mugs. "And what's new about that?" She asked. "I've never known you to be exactly sober at eleven o'clock on a Saturday night. It's only a matter of degree"

I sat up in the couch and she snuggled in beside me with the two mugs and watched the end of Cilla Black.

"The things people do to get onto television" she grunted as the show ended. "Will you move now and get yourself washed. I think you should wear your blue shirt and your new jeans. You have the cutest little bum in them new jeans. I'll be the envy of every wan in the place, with a big man like ye."

I went into the bathroom, shaved, showered and prettied myself up.

"Well, aren't you the handsome bugger." She exclaimed as I represented myself in the living room. "Midnight in Moore Street." She was, of course, referring to the new aftershave she'd bought me for my birthday.

She was curled up on the couch like a cat that had the cream and it was all I could do not to leap on her bones and ravish her there and then. Instead, I shuffled up to her and snuggled into her throat, necking shamelessly.

"Get off me you big galoot." She screamed. "You'll ruin me make-up." But the giggling and thrashing of her only prompted me to further action and we both parted, hot and flushed, about five minutes later.

"Aren't you the little devil," she retorted. "I'm after spending the last hour slaving in front of a mirror with me make up brush. And it only takes two minutes for you to ruin it all."

She busied herself happily in front of the mirror and I put on the kettle for a coffee.

"It's a lovely flat Moira has. You'll only love it." She said between strokes. "I was up inside of it last Wednesday after work. It's only gorgeous."

With half an ear I listened to her describing the big living room, the balcony looking out onto the big back garden, and the three ENORMOUS bedrooms, each with big Victorian windows.

I was only half listening because the guy on the TV was on his fifth question and was going for £32,000. He still had his 'ask a friend', his 'fifty fifty' and his 'ask the audience', and he was looking good for it. So it came as a bit of a surprise when Marian started talking about a guy being murdered downstairs.

"What? Here?" I exclaimed. "When?"

"Ben Morris, you're not listening to a word I'm saying. Are you? It's not here. It's downstairs from Mary's new flat. Some poor guy was stabbed to death in his own living room. His body wasn't found for a week. Apparently, the shock put the people before Mary right off the place and that's why they moved."

Now she had my FULL attention. I was agape.

"Wha'? Killed downstairs?" I must have been white as a ghost.

Completely misreading my reaction, Marian laughed in my face. "There's no ghost. You scaredy cat. According to the landlord it was a blessing in disguise. He'd been trying to clear the flat upstairs for ages and this was just playing right into his hands.

The guy that was murdered was no angel either apparently. A right little sheister by all accounts. Was at least two months behind in his rent when he left."

She laughed at the disrespect of it all.

"Anyway, they've been there for a fortnight and there's been no bumps in the night... So you've nothing to fear from ghosts."

She gave me a playful thump on my shoulder and disappeared into the bathroom.

I sat, my head reeling, staring at the TV, seeing nothing, hearing nothing. My ears were ringing and my mind racing.

I hadn't been near the place since that day. I hadn't been on the street and subconsciously avoided being in the vicinity at all.

In my mind I saw the street, the walking to it and the walking from it. It was as if I wouldn't go INTO the house, but my mind wouldn't travel past the street.

Then I was standing outside the flat in the quite pathway, and then I was in the room again.

He was behind me... dead.

Boy George was on the radio...

And suddenly Marian burst from the bathroom shouting "C'mon Tele Addict. Get your coat on. We'd better go."

I heard the TV again, and the sound of her moving around the flat, and reality started filtering in again.

"Just a sec. I'll just use the bog before we go."

I lashed into the bathroom and closed the door behind me. I was sweating and cold. I looked at myself in the mirror over the sink and I saw the wild eyes beginning to calm down. Or was I imagining it? Was I just used to it?

I splashed water on my face and sat for a while on the side of the bath with the towel in my face, my head resting on my hands. It was warm and comfortable and safe.

I sat for a while and then heard Marian hammering on the door. "C'mon Ben, what's keeping you?"

"I'll be just a minute," I shouted back. "Where's your patience?"

With a quick look in the mirror, assuring myself I looked normal again, I left the bathroom, grabbed my coat off the rack on the wall, ran out of the flat and yelled into the living room.

"Here I am. Waiting in the hall. Women. Are they ever ready?"

Giving me a thump as she loped out the door, Marian raced ahead of me down the stairs and I locked the flat behind us.

She linked me as we turned out the gate and looked up into my eyes. "I'm really looking forward to tonight," she said. "It seems ages since we were out together with the gang."

She had completely forgotten about the murdered guy in the flat. To her it was no more than an incidental detail about her friends flat. She had no idea what she had told me and I realised that I had completely over-reacted. As luck would have it she hadn't noticed, but that was luck. I had to be careful next time around.

"Mmmm. It has been a while all right. In fact, I can't remember when the last time this gang of us were together. It must have been after the holidays in Malaga."

"God, is it that long?" She was genuinely shocked. "There was a time we used get together almost every Friday night." She thought for a bit as we went down the road. "God, they were the days weren't they. What a laugh they were. It was as if we had no troubles in the world. Now it seems we have nothing but troubles."

We both laughed at that. "A few pints will change that," I said, and we both laughed again.

Before long we were walking through Ranelagh village and in the corner doors of McSorleys. The welcoming buzz of the pub met us and the familiar smell of the wood and beer wrapped itself around us and led us around the pub until we found a few of the others in a grand big section of the pub

It wasn't long before the pints were flowing and the conversation was flying from one topic to the other. Not surprisingly the most popular conversation was the 'Dead Man Downstairs' as he came to be known. Such a range of stories were circulating that it was fascinating just to notice the imagination of people being applied to the event.

It would appear that Bert was hacked to death with a bowie knife, his blood smeared all over the flat, with rude words on each wall. He was a well-known homosexual, who had been into kinky sex that had gone too far. Having been buggered by at least 15 crazed bikers, he was then ritually and brutally dismembered, his limbs (with bite marks on the tenderest parts) scattered throughout the flat... even in his bed, the oven and the bidet. He had died of an overdose of pills, peacefully in his bed. He had slit his wrists in the bath, because everybody knew it was a suicide. He had hung himself in the kitchen and the landlady found him hanging there from the lightbulb when she turned on the lights (the place being dark because he had closed all the curtains). He had been stabbed in the throat, eyes, and they had finally plunged the knife into his heart.

He had been tortured systematically, using cigarettes, long needles, a surgeon's scalpel, and thumbscrews, before being left to die, tied to the bed with his lifeblood dripping from his toes.

As the night went on the stories got wilder and wilder and by eleven o'clock I was telling variations of what I'd heard to an appreciative audience. I was describing the state of the place, with blood dripping from the counters, when Moira passed by and listened to the story.

"Ben Morris" she said disparagingly, "Where do you get off? He was found on the couch with a single knife wound. Will you stop making up stories, scaring people off my party. People are beginning to think they are coming back to a house of horrors. Will you give it a rest."

With that she moved on to the next group of people, spreading the same story, quenching the grisly tales threatening to engulf the good mood of the party.

"Well," I said, "I guess she'd know… she lives there." I giggled, hiding my hurt at the reprimand. Of course she was right…. And I was probably the only person at the party who knew that for sure.

After that there was little talk of the 'Dead Man Downstairs', especially if any of the three girls were around.

Later on, just as last pints were being called, Moira approached me at the bar. "Listen Ben, I'm sorry for pulling you up earlier on, but it was getting out of hand. One or two of the younger ones from work were nearly going home. They were scared out of their minds."

"Go on?"

"Mmm, seriously. The thought of going to the house that was…" and she paused for effect, waving her fingers in the air to denote italics, "dripping with blood… was beginning to terrify them."

"Lord, I'm sorry Moira. I just got carried away with the absurdity of the thing." Suddenly I realised what I was saying, what I had been talking about all night. It had all become so unreal… like a game, that the reality of it, of Bert sitting dead on the couch, had disappeared a long time ago. It was as if we were in a Murder Mystery weekend and none of it was for real.

"Don't worry about it Ben. We were all at it. It just got out of hand." Looking at me strangely she said it again. "Honestly Ben… It's OK."

Seeing her concern, I snapped out of my reverie and laughed. "Too much drink, I guess. What are you having?"

"No. I'm OK. I'm in a round. Get in there before the night is over altogether."

We scrambled for our last drinks and I made my way back to Marian.

"How you doing sunshine? Here's a refill." I said as I sat down on a spare seat beside Marian.

"Where have you been all night?" she asked. "Up to no good I suppose. I saw you having quiet words with Moira. What was that all about?"

"Oh, nothing at all. She told me off earlier for telling horror stories and wanted to make her peace. How have you been doing. Anybody trying to get into yer nickers?"

"You galoot. They all know I'm all yours. Nobody wants to go near me now." She leant over and gave me a big kiss on the cheek. "You lucky bugger."

"We'll have less of that, you two," said Mary coming over to us. "Save it for later back in the flat. We're all heading back now. Are yez coming?"

"Be with you in a minute." Said Marian. "We'll just finish off these two and we'll be after you."

"D'ye know where the place is?"

We both nodded... and suddenly I realised I shouldn't know.

"I was over there with Moira on Wednesday," said Marian. "I can surely find it again."

"Just follow the noise. You're sure to find us. See you there."

Mary headed off with a big crowd and we were left on our own for a moment.

"I love you, Ben Morris." said Marian after a few moments, looking drunkenly into my eyes. "You're the best boyfriend in the world."

"The feeling is quite mutual, Marian Howard. I would follow you to the ends of the world."

"Oh, you old romantic."

"Less of the old please… did you get the drink?"

"I did" she said laughing. "The practical romantic. Let's go and get down to the party before they have all the food gone. I've got a fierce dose of the nibblies on me."

"You're not the only one. The coats. On with the coats. And let's be gone."

We stumbled out of the pub, laughing as we snuggled together and headed down the quiet lane towards Beechwood Road.

We turned up Dunville Avenue and it was as if it was a physical shock to walk up towards the house. There was an almost inhuman force pushing me away and the nearer we got the stronger it became.

I tried to ignore it, chatting away with Marian, but eventually she stopped talking, looked at me and asked, "Are you all right Ben? You don't look too well."

"No. No. I'm grand. I guess I'm just hungry." I tried to laugh it off, pretending nothing was happening, but it wasn't really working. I felt sick, nauseous, and not a little shaky.

"You know which house it is?" I asked as we moved towards the house.

"The one with all the noise, I guess," she said laughing.

Just then a crowd piled out of a taxi pulled up outside the house. Marian knew them all and there was a mad scramble of hugs, kisses and hellos. In all the fuss I sat back on the wall of the garden, my back against the railings.

The thought of going up that path, that nice quiet secluded path, was making me nauseous. If I could avoid it at all I would have, but there was no way out.

"Ben, have you met Tony and Ger? They work with me and started going out with each other only last Saturday. Isn't that WONDERFUL."

I looked at Tony and Ger and nodded my wonderment. The darkness and the alcohol, I hope, obscured the lack of wonderment in my face.

"Nice to meet you guys, eh..." I faltered... Marian had moved on... "You guys work with Marian? In the same room like?"

It was feeble, but it worked.

"No," Tony laughed. "In the same Department. Marian works downstairs from me... And upstairs from Ger." He laughed, and smiled at Ger. "It's all a bit complicated really, but the department is spread over a whole building."

"Ah, I get it. It's the same for me. There's about three hundred working in our place, and we're spread over about five floors." I laughed, and before we knew it we were up the stairs to the front door and making our way through the massive big front hall.

"In to the left, in to the left," shouted Mary, who was shepherding people from the front door into the party proper. "There's food in the kitchen. Straight through... Follow the smell."

There was a great buzz about the place and in the kitchen there was a massive spread of canapés, sandwiches and finger bowls filled with crisps and peanuts. I helped myself to some sandwiches, filling my mouth with canapés as I moved along the table.

"Trust you, Ben Morris. I should have known. Wherever there's free food I'll find you there." Marian cuddled up beside me and took one of the sandwiches I had and delicately, almost coyly, nibbled at it.

"Oh, Marian. You can be so cruel sometimes. It must be weeks since you fed me."

"Mary, where should I hide this drink?" she hollered at Mary in particular, but really at anyone who lived in the flat since Mary was nowhere to be seen.

Moira came over and took the bag from her. "I'll put it over beside the fridge. It'll be there when you need it. Would you like one now? I have some cold in the fridge."

"Would I what?" I mumbled through another canapé.

"That'd be great Moira," said Marian. "You must have been killed all day putting this together?"

"To put it mildly," said Moira, "And it'll take your man there about five minutes to put it all away."

I attempted to look offended, but the two of them were so enjoying the jibe that I let it go and stretched for a few cocktail sausages I hadn't seen earlier.

Moira returned with two cold cans of beer and we ambled back into the living room. The place was quite crowded by now and someone had turned up the music. By the looks of things there had been a few people who had come a lot earlier and were comfortably ensconced in the sofas and armchairs. Around the walls and here and there on the floor there were chairs and bean bags.

All in all it was a great set-up. Suddenly Mary was behind us.

"Well Ben, do you want the guided tour? You look as if you're appraising the place with an estate agents' eye."

I was embarrassed, but she insisted. "Seriously, Let's take a look around. Marian has seen it all before. Let me do the honours. I'm just dying to show it off."

A little mollified I followed her out into the hall and through the three bedrooms. There was a massive double door between Mary and Moira's rooms, and the third bedroom was down the back in the return. It wasn't so large as the other two, "but what it lacks in size it make up for in privacy," said Mary, laughing. "You can hear just about everything through those doors. If you fancy a night of passion you make sure you leave the radio on."

The windows were fantastic, looking out on the front garden and the back garden. "So much light," said Marian, "Just flooding in." My eyes were glued to the view of the front path leading up to the house and around to the side entrance.

"Come on and see the back bedroom," called Mary. "And I'll show you the bathroom as well. You'll need it before the night is out." She was in her element, loving the role of Lady of the Manor.

"The toilets are here on the right, under the stairs, and the bathroom is here on the left, just beside Gillian's bedroom, which as you can see is a little smaller than the other two.

We all stood at the door, not wishing to invade Gillian's space, but having a good gawk anyway.

"It's great Mary. How ever did you find the place?" I said as we made our way back to the living room.

"It was in the newspaper. Gillian, God Bless her, stood for the afternoon and met the Landlord when he arrived. She poured on all the charm and when she thought she had it in the bag she finally convinced him by saying she'd arrange for the two of us to come, there and then, to show ourselves."

She looked at us with her most matronly look. "And I think that THAT was what got it for us. Being willing to get up and be there to show ourselves to be decent and upright people... with jobs, of course."

We all nodded sagely and agreed that speed was of the essence in these things, that it was a travesty the difficulty there was in trying to secure a flat in Dublin these days.

"Weren't you so lucky to find a place like this," said Marian. "And the landlord? What's he like?"

"Oh, salt of the earth. Wants no trouble. Just wanted decent people in who would take care of the place and pay the rent. No trouble, he kept saying. Not like that sheister he had downstairs."

Suddenly I was back in reality again. Suddenly I knew where I was again. I felt weak and dizzy.

We were back in the big room with all the music, talking and laughing. The lights had been dimmed and there was loads of activity going on. I moved over to the big window looking out at the front garden.

For a moment I could see two figures coming up from the gate and going around to the side door. I knew they weren't there, but I could feel them there again. I wished they stopped there and one of them hadn't gone in, had faltered at the last minute and gone home...

Standing there, wishing, I then saw me coming out with the Marigolds on. Not running, not looking back. Perfectly ordinary except for those Marigolds.

"It's a lovely view, isn't it." Marian was standing behind me, her arms curling around my waist.

"Lovely," I said. "Lovely."

"D'ye wanna dance, mister?" she mimicked, changing mood with the song. "I love this one. C'me on."

She pulled me out through the people on the floor and we danced to "I just wanna dance, dance with my baby" by I have no idea who. When we were spent she pulled me into the kitchen and we rooted for more beer.

The kitchen was getting lively. There was great praise for the place and Mary was in her element.

"But there's a place going free downstairs. Well, not free... but reasonable." She laughed at the joke. "The Landlord is looking for someone to take it over and told us if we know of anybody to let him know."

There were knowing nods around the room. What we all knew was anybody's guess, but I guess alcohol had a lot to do with it.

Mary was getting into saleswoman pitch now. "Say, why don't we go down and have a look at it now? He's left the door open... expressly so that we can show people around."

Personally, I would rather have had my eyelashes burnt off with a flame-thrower than follow her down to that flat, but there was a swell of curiosity surging through the kitchen and suddenly the door to the hall was opened and we were all gushing down the stairs to the basement flat. Marian was walking directly behind me, her arms holding my waist. There was no way out.

I thought a trip to the loo, but no, there was someone in there. We passed down the stairs and Mary switched on the light to the bottom of the stairs.

"This is where the house phone was and, before we came, everybody had access to it. But the Landlord says he will move it upstairs and get a separate phone for the basement flat.

"This door would normally be locked when there's someone living in here, but for now..." and with a flourish she pushed open the door and showed us the darkness inside.

"Lights," she called, and switched on the lighting.

The flat below was bathed in a bright yellow light. We all filed off the stairway and into the room.

I was amazed. It was totally different. Nothing was the same. It was bright and airy, whereas before it had been old and, well... used. All the furniture was new and in different places. The sink had moved to the other wall and the units were all new and fitted to the wall. The colour of the walls had all changed and the floor was half tiles and half wooden designer floor.

My amazement must have been obvious and Mary immediately hopped on it.

"Isn't it just gorgeous, Ben. Wouldn't you just love to live here."

Under the circumstances I couldn't think of anything
I'd love less, but instead I agreed, saying it was a
beautiful flat.

We all crowded around the couch, a bright green
modern cotton affair with big overstuffed cushions
that just begged to be fallen into. It faced into the
new wooden fireplace with a gas fire effect
arrangement in the center.

"He must be asking a fortune for the place" said Ger,
the girl from the office.

"Apparently not," said the saleswoman, "All he wants
is a good tenant who will look after the place and pay
the rent."

They all looked around speculatively.

"Any takers?"

We all laughed and we were quickly shown the
bedroom and the bathroom and trooped back up the
stairs.

"Would you be interested?" asked Marian as we went
back into the kitchen.

"Cool it Ben. Cool it." I thought.

"I dunno. Would you?"

"No, I think you're right. It would be a bit much living downstairs from this lot. We'd have no privacy at all."

I laughed... and then the meaning of what she'd said sank in. *We'd* have no privacy? Maybe I was jumping to conclusions.

Suddenly we were dancing again, but this time it was a slow song and Marian was nicely cuddled into me, her head leaning on my chest.

I couldn't get over the change in the room. It was as if the old room, the scene of the crime, had never existed. It was as if Bert never existed.

Now he was just a story, and not a very accurate one, that was told in pubs and parties. Nothing remained of the man or the manner.

The music changed.

And suddenly it was Frieda's song...

the guitar music...

"You drink your coffee, and... I sip my tea, and we're... sitting here... playing so cool, thinking what will be will be...

I move a little closer to you... not knowing quite what to do...

The sax

...And then we touch, much too much, this moment has been waiting for a long long time...

...Shiver, makes me quiver...

...is it something you've been waiting for...

...sing it to me in the silent tongue....

...or will you just politely say good night...

And the sax....

and the silence.....

And the drums ....

And the sax.....

Marian and I danced, but I was in Limerford, I was in a flat in Ranelagh, I was alone in my mind with my memories.

Nothing remained of the man or the manner... nowhere but in my head.

Chapter 7

They had been looking at him strange from the moment he walked into the pub. He was sure of it.

"No. It couldn't be," he reassured himself. "It's my imagination."

He walked up to the gang of them, smiling and they smiling in return. "How's it going lads?"

They all hailed him and when he saw their glasses were all full or nearly full he nodded to the glasses saying, "You're all ok for drink? I'll get meself a pint." and headed for the bar.

There weren't many at the bar so he caught the barman's eye quick enough and ordered a pint of Guinness. While he stood waiting he glanced back at the lads. Was it his imagination or were they all, one by one, glancing over at him. They were talking about him, he was sure of it.

The barman came with his pint, he paid for it and went back over to the lads.

It was as if the conversation died for a second.

Seamus saved it, rather badly. "We were just talking about this guy who was stabbed in his flat. He was from your end of the country wasn't he?"

Were they all looking at him, gauging him for a reaction?

"Is that right now? I hadn't heard that."

"Aye. A Limerford man. About our own age I believe."

"Is that so? I haven't heard much about it at all."

They were baiting him now, playing with him.

"Did anyone hear his name? Or anything else about him?" He'd play them at his own game. Fuckers!

He was surprised how calm he was. He hadn't gone to pieces like he did when Marian mentioned it to him. He must be coming inured to it. Is this how it was all going to happen for him? A hard bastard.

"Devil a bit else. Just that he was a Limerford man."

"And our own age," added Tom.

There was a brief pause in the conversation.

"And a bit of a nasty bastard by the sound of things. I was talking to Marian recently and she tells me he was a few months behind in his rent when he kicked it. Story has it that the Landlord had been trying to get rid of him for a while before… events caught up with him"

They all laughed at Billy's hiccup of words and the conversation flowed again. Contributions came from all angles as to what theories were about the place and rumours circulating.

Eventually the conversation veered off on a different angle and Ben found himself in a side conversation with Tom.

"It's funny you hadn't heard of the guy who was killed," Tom was saying. "Limerford's not such a big place, is it?"

"It's not really, and I'd say I know just about every man Jack and Mary in it. It's just that I haven't heard much about this murder and I haven't been talking to anyone at home about it. I've no doubt I know whoever it turns out to be, but I've not heard who it is yet."

Tom looked at him with what seemed to be a slightly suspicious, if disbelieving look. "There's a story going around that his name was Bert and he went to the same school as you." He let that sit for a bit.

It was like a slap in the face. His blood began to pound in his head. He could feel his face going scarlet. This was definitely a prize piece of baiting.

"Aye, I knew a guy called Bert in Limerford, all right. Didn't have much to do with him though. Is that who you hear it might be?" He said, stalling for time.

He could sense the other conversation waning as the other lads strained to hear what they were saying.

"That's who they say it was all right… And they also say you were seen with him on the week-end of the murder."

"And who'd be saying this? I ask you." He realised he was raising his voice, but he couldn't help himself. He tried to regain his initial detachment. "Who would have seen such a thing?"

"Are you saying you didn't see Bert on the week-end he was murdered?" Tom was so calm it was frightening. He had obviously thought this one through. It was no accident that he was sitting here alone in a crowd with him.

Ben suddenly remembered that Tom was a Garda. With that realisation his composure dropped completely. He looked at the rest of the lads and saw that they had stopped their conversation completely and they were openly staring at them, waiting for him to reply.

He looked at the door of the pub and calculated how many people he would have to push past to get to it and realised how unlikely it was that he would make it out unhindered.

He felt like a cornered rat and was certain he looked like one too. His guilt was written all over his face. He could no longer hide it from these people.

They knew him and knew when he was as deep in dudu as a man could be.

Could he plead with them for cover, for mercy, for silence? Could he lean on their friendship?

Still he felt he could brazen it out.

"I haven't seen Bert in ages. I didn't even know he was in Dublin. I'd heard he was working in London." He waited a minute to calm down having said it. "But if you say it was him was killed, you'd know best, being on the inside track as they say."

"Aye, the inside track has you in it too though. It appears there's a video camera saw the two of you together in Rathmines Shopping Centre on the morning of the murder. I seen it myself. It was you all right."

Ben could sense Tom going in for the kill. There was no comeback from this. It was out now. They had evidence. He was trapped. The other lads were openly gaping at the exchange.

The blood pounded in his temples. He could feel the bile rising in this throat. He was wet with sweat....

I woke up sweating in the bed, my blood rushing and my breath coming in quick rushed gasps. The sheets were drenched and my hair was wet, stuck to my head. I was breathing deeply.

Chapter 8

It was a pretty normal Wednesday morning in the office.

I had arrived in at about ten past nine and the place was still half-empty. Rows and rows of desks and only the odd one inhabited.

There were days I hated this place, with the musty steel filing cabinets and the old wooden desks. There were other days I loved the comfortable antiquity of the place with its views out to the sports fields and the ancient sycamores and chestnut trees surrounding the fields.

This morning it had been a lovely walk up the tree lined avenue to the old building. The air was clean and fresh and there was a crisp spring feeling about the day that put a slight bounce in my step and a smile on my face.

I had got off the bus on the Mobhi Road and walked back to the gates of the demesne. I could hear the canal flowing under the bridge and smell the dank odour of undergrowth. I do believe I even saw a fox on the way up the drive, as well as the few squirrels I sometimes see when the weather is not completely awful. The sky was clear and blue and there was no hint of cloud or wind. It was beautiful and I breathed in with that healthy enthusiasm such a day inspires.

I settled myself at my desk and for a while looked out the big window at the sports field. There was nobody about and the sun glistened on the grass. I remembered the schoolteacher at school making us learn off a line of Irish which we were to 'make sure to include' into an essay or composition or answer in some way or other. "Bhí druacht na maidine ag gliscerni mar phearlaí ar an feir glass". Literally translated it means "The morning dew was glistening like pearls on the green grass" and somehow or other we were to include it into our work to show our command of the language. The truth was that our command of the language was so basic, and indeed our poetic ability so drab that a line like this would glisten like a pearl in a pig sty. But hope sprang eternal and we all learnt it off.

As it happened, I couldn't find a way of including it into my dissertation on the change Daniel O'Connell made to Irish politics…. Or maybe I did mention how he came out of his house one morning and his love of Ireland was so strong that it was only strengthened by the morning dew glistening like pearls on the green grass. I thought about it as I gazed absently out the window, but it's so long ago now I cannot remember for sure.

Harry arrived in with the morning papers and left the Irish Times on Jeff's desk. I knew Jeff wouldn't be in today so I wandered over to the coffee machine, picking up the paper as I passed his desk, and made myself a strong Mocha.

Nothing scandalous on the front page. The coffee machine chugged away as I flipped the paper under my arm and stood staring out the window. What a beautiful day. I heard someone behind me and turned to see who it was.

"Hi Roger. Nice day? What?"

"Absolutely fantastic. I was cycling over the new bridge on the way in and the view out to sea is only breath-taking. I really felt like stopping and just breathing it in for an hour or two. It was so fantastic. The sun low in the sky and the clear blue of the sky and the sea. Wonderful. Absolutely wonderful."

He swooned on for a bit longer as I picked up my coffee and moved aside to let him at the machine.

"It's funny how we still call that the new bridge, even though it's over ten years old at this stage."

"Yea," he laughed. "Though I suppose it is new in comparison to the other ones. I suppose we'll have to call it by its real name when the twisted one gets built. Though that'll probably be called the Twisted Bridge from the start."

I wandered back to my desk and spread the newspaper out over the other papers scattered over it. I scanned the front page and seeing nothing special turned over the page.

It leapt out at me like as if it was the only thing written on the page.

"Killer found in Ranelagh Murder"

My heart suddenly beat so fast it hurt and my face felt red hot. Inside I felt sick. Suddenly I was cold and hot and sweating.

> "There has been a major advance in the Ranelagh Murder Enquiry yesterday when a man was arrested in connection with the murder. He is described as in his forties and a friend of the family of the dead man.
>
> Previous enquiries into the murder had led Gardaí to believe that this might have been a cult killing or a part of a suicide pact. While the circumstances surrounding the death were peculiar, no motive for a murder could be established and no evidence of anybody else at the scene of the death could be found.
>
> However, in a dramatic shift in the case, yesterday afternoon the man arrested was overheard talking in a public house in Rathmines that he had 'killed a guy in Ranelagh'. The barman immediately called the Gardaí who arrested the man.
>
> It is expected the man will appear before Rathmines District Court later this morning."

I didn't know whether to laugh or to cry. It was so absurd.

Who could it possibly be and what was this guy up to. I read the article again… and again.

By now my pulse had returned to normal but I felt sick and cold. My coffee sat cold on the desk beside me. I tasted it and put it to one side.

I read the article again.

I went to get another coffee, closing the newspaper before I left the desk in case anybody would pass by and see what I had been reading.

Roger was still in the kitchen.

"What? Another coffee already? Are you all right Ben? You look a bit pale." He looked concerned and moved in my direction as if to examine my health all the better.

"No. No. I'm fine," I muttered. "Must be the week-end catching up."

"We were just saying that they seem to have caught someone for that Ranelagh Murder." said Mick, who was standing behind me.

I swung around so quickly I nearly threw the mug of cold coffee all over Mick, who was standing behind the door when I came in, so I hadn't seen him.

"Hey, watch it. You nearly drowned me," he laughed as the coffee splashed onto the floor.

I grabbed a handful of kitchen towel and threw it on the floor over the spilt coffee.

"Sorry, I didn't see you there. You gave me a bit of a fright." By now I was rightly rattled. I tried to cover it up, mopping up the coffee, my foot wiping the kitchen towel over the floor.

"What's that you were saying? They found a murderer?"

"Yup. Looks like the guy was bragging in Slattery's yesterday afternoon that he had cut the guy up good and proper," said Roger.

I threw the towel into the bin and washed out my cup in the sink.

"Wow," I muttered, my concentration on the cleaning of the cup.

"Yea," Mick took up the story. "It was all about the place last night. I was in The Hill and nobody was talking about anything else. Seems they'd been drinking together and fell out over something and he took the knife and carved him up good. The way it was told in The Hill he was little short of hacking his head off with an axe."

We all laughed.

An image of Bert sitting in the chair holding the knife flashed through my mind.

And he looked so neat and tidy. Clean and intact. Not mutilated beyond recognition.

"This was the Ranelagh Murder?" I asked. "The one a couple of months ago?"

"The very one. Four weeks later the guy ups and confesses. And to the whole of Slattery's by the sounds of it."

"But I didn't think it was a hatchet job. I thought he'd been written off as a suicide?" I almost pleaded.

"Not by the looks of it now. Seems it was a bloodbath." Mick was getting into it now. "Skin and hair flying all over the place. A massive fight and load of blood and guts."

I was about to contradict him, to tell him there was no evidence of anybody else at the scene, but I noticed Roger was looking at me strangely.

Was it obvious that I was acting strange? Did I look guilty?

"There wasn't a wall on the place that wasn't covered in blood. The more people you talked to in The Hill the gorier the fight became. Apparently, yer man in Slatterys was pretty graphic in his descriptions."

I filled my cup with coffee again.

"The things you do when you're drunk," I muttered as I left the kitchen, pretending to be pre-occupied with something back at my desk. "See you later."

My mind was going haywire. Images of Rogers face flashed before me. Then the knife in Bert's hand. Then the descriptions Mick was painting.

I felt sick and uncomfortable. Out of the corner of my eye I say Roger leaving the kitchen and coming towards me. I lifted a file off my tray stack and opened it busily on my desk. As if it were very pressing and important, I flicked through the pages in the file and dragged a note pad into range and doodled some scribbled notes on the page as I flicked.

Roger passed my desk without stopping and I nonchalantly sipped my coffee as I pored purposefully through the folder. Without lifting my head from the folder, I observed Roger until he got to his desk. He never looked back or glanced in my direction.

I was over-reacting. It was all in my head. I was panicking.

"Calm down Ben," I thought. "It's cool. Everything is OK"

I closed up the file in front of me and looked at the cover. It was an old accounts file that Jeff had left on my desk the previous afternoon. He was finished with it and didn't know where to put it.

I picked it up and went downstairs to file it in the archives. I always enjoy the trip to Archives. It's such a long walk through the big old corridors, down the magnificent old staircases and through the grand reception area.

The cubby box for the Porter ruins the effect of the main hall, but if you let your mind ignore its tacky presence you can imagine it as it was, as it should be. The supreme elegance of the building seeped into me as I rounded the last corner and entered the narrow confines of the basement vaults.

"Morning Bernadette," I smiled at Miss Caruana as I entered the small office that guarded the Archives.

"Good morning, Ben," she smiled back, beaming at me as if I were her White Knight on a horse come to present her with a box of Milk Tray. "Isn't it a beautiful morning."

"It certainly is. You know, I saw a fox on the way up the drive this morning."

"Yes, that would be Russel. I noticed him yesterday evening and I leaving on my bicycle to go home. A fine looking character he is. Up to no good I'll say."

"Indeed yes."

"Like yourself no doubt." She grinned mischievously at me and if she weren't well past sixty years of age and hardly able to lift herself off the seat I would have been worried for my long lost virginity.

Studiously ignoring the flirtation, I slid the folder on the desk.

"Oh, there's none of that in my life Bernadette, to be sure." We both laughed conspiratorially. "Jeff asked me to give you back this file. Will you take care of it for me?"

She picked up the file as if it were a warm mohair cardigan in Arnott's, feeling its texture and quality. Rubbing her hand over the cover, she read the label on the front.

"Oh, I will Ben. I will. You just leave it with me." Her eyes looked at me faithfully as if I had just entrusted her with my life's savings. She held the folder to her chest and hugged it close.

"I will so, thanks a million," I said and turned to leave the room.

"Have a nice day, Ben. May God watch over you. You're such a nice lad."

I looked back at her, and the sense of sincerity just flowed out of her.

"Sure, you're not too bad yourself," I said, leaving, and heard her cackle merrily to herself at the implied compliment.

As I came into the main hall I bumped into George Lucas, who was working with me on a contract for stationery.

"Did you get the Tender in yet from York?" I asked as I passed him.

"I did," he replied. "But I'm not sure how far we can go with it at the moment. We're expecting a few more in during the week and as soon as we get them we'll be able to proceed."

"But we know we're going to go ahead with York. Why do we have to wait for the rest of the Tenders to proceed?"

"You know the way it is Ben. We can't…"

We got into a big discussion on the rights and wrongs of red tape and before I knew it I was scribbling furiously at my desk and it was half past twelve.

"You going for lunch?"

Roger was standing over my desk with his coat in his hand. "I'm off around to The Tolka. D'ye wanna come over?"

"God, is it that time already? Sure. I'll be right with you. Just giv's a minute to finish this bit."

"I'm off to the jax. I'll meet you in the Main Hall."
He said as he walked off.

"See you there."

Five minutes later we were walking by the canal
towards The Tolka House.

"You seem mighty busy this morning." He smirked
as we crossed over the road.

"You know the way it is... Once you get started on
something it's hard to lift your head. I got talking to
George this morning and one thing led to another.
Suddenly you're in the middle of a can of worms and
everything is wriggling all over the place."

"When I saw the look of concentration on your face
this morning coming back with me coffee I thought
you'd lost the wages file for the whole of the Civil
Service and were trying to re-write it before lunch-
time."

We laughed. "No, nothing as deadly as all that. Just
a Stationery Contract."

Under the laugh a drift of uneasiness began to shift in
my soul. Maybe the word 'deadly' was appropriate
and maybe it was more deadly than losing the wages
file, not less. I shuddered despite the warm
atmosphere in the pub.

With a plate of Beef and Mushroom pie, peas and chips in front of us, we launched into a full-scale review of the match the previous night. Wiping our plates, we asked the girl for two coffees and sat back in our seats.

"What a fine place this is. There's a few Friday sessions in here that'll go down in history." He proclaimed as we watched the girl taking away the plates.

"Aye, and quite a few that we couldn't remember the following morning."

"Probably more of them forgotten that way, if the truth be known." Roger had been in the Service for about fifteen years and was about as settled into the routine as anyone could be. He did his job and went home to his wife and two kids, and enjoyed both lives for what they were. His job was to get money to allow his family survive.

He loved his wife Margaret, and didn't see any life beyond making her happy and bringing up Philip and Georgina to be good little people… if they wanted to be. He was much of the belief that people were what they wanted to be and it was not up to him to interfere. If his kids grew up to be thugs then so be it. He wouldn't necessarily like it, but that'd be their choice, not his.

The girl brought us our coffees and we chatted for a while, letting the food settle inside us.

"Will you be along for the session this Friday?" he asked. "Frank Heffernan is retiring and a few of the old cronies will be getting together."

"I'll make me mind up on that on Friday, I'd say. It depends on who's coming over, to be honest." We got up to leave. "Marian is meeting up with crowd out of her work and I said I might join her for a few."

"Did you ever work with Frank?" he asked as we left the pub.

"I didn't. There was talk of it once, when I was just after joining, but the penny fell the other way and it never happened."

"He's a gas man, you know. I worked with him for a few years in the eighties. Got his head well screwed on, he has. Bought a lot of property when he was younger, when prices were cheap, and did the places up. Stories have it he has about ten properties about town and himself and the missus have them all rented out. She does the rent collecting and organises the maintenance and such. Some of the stories he would tell. He was a funny man."

"Well, I didn't know that," I said. "I always figured him for a bit of a duffer. A foostery old character. Looks can be deceiving I suppose."

"Dead right they can. And a bigger deceiver you'll not get than Frank. As shrewd a guy as you'll get. Got his head screwed on tight he has."

We walked along the path beside the canal admiring the view and as we were crossing the road to the grounds he broke the reverie.

"Did you know it was in one of his properties that guy was killed in Ranelagh."

Unknown to him, my heart nearly stopped.

"What?"

"Aye, it was his missus that found the dead body. You should have heard him the following morning. Apparently, his missus was in bits for weeks afterwards. She's not been right since. The names he called that little runt for getting himself killed in his flat. There's no doubt in his mind that the guy brought it on himself, and the fact he did it in his house is a source of great aggravation to Frank"

"Aye, it would be," I said, but the words were mechanical. I was thinking of Frank's missus finding Bert dead on the couch and the shock it must have been.

We arrived at the main door and I opened it up and ushered Roger through.

"A wee word of warning. Don't mention it at the booze up on Friday. It's still a sore point and it's best left out of it."

I grunted assent behind him as we climbed the great stairs and turned into our office.

Slightly breathless I put away my overcoat and sat back at my desk.

That was one booze-up I might give a miss.

I opened the Stationery File and began to work on the York Contract.

Chapter 9

"Are you going over to The Tolka, Ben?"

It was Roger and he was heading over to Frank's Booze Up. I had been talking to Marian earlier in the afternoon and she was heading into Neary's with the crowd out of work. I told her I'd join her later, but for some reason I didn't want to be waiting in the Bar when they arrived.

"Aye, I'll be over shortly. I just want to finish up this."

"Will you be long, or will I wait for ye?" he asked.

"I'll be about two minutes, so if you'd drop this over in the Out Tray for me I'll be ready when you get back," I said, handing him a handful of envelopes I'd spent the afternoon getting ready for the post.

I finished up what I was doing and minutes later we were making our way along the canal path to the Tolka House. It was warm and friendly inside, with a big crowd from the office congregated beside the bar.

"What'll you have lads?" asked Frank as we got nearer the group.

"I'll have a pint," said Roger.

"Same for me thanks Frank," I said, nodding hellos to the rest of the lads.

"Two Guinness," shouted Frank to the barman, turning back to us.

"End of an era, Frank," said Roger, clapping him on the back. "Not many of your gang left at this stage, is there?"

"Indeed there's not, Roger. After me there's only Paddy Cumiskey, and he only has another month to go."

"Is that right? I thought he was long gone. I haven't seen him in years."

"Nobody has," laughed Frank. "He's been out sick for as long as I can remember, but they're moving him from sick pay to a pension from the end of next month."

We all laughed at the irony of it. Last out of his generation, but out to farm before his peers.

"I do drop over to him from time to time," continued Frank. "He started in the Service the same day as I did. We worked together for a while and then got shifted over the years to different locations. But we always kept in touch. I remember when we were both up in Kildare Street..."

Frank launched into a story and the barman signalled that our pints were ready. Without even stalling in his narrative, Frank passed us over the two pints, nodded acknowledgement at our thanks, and took another sup out of his own pint.

With half an ear to Frank I looked around the pub. It was the usual motley crowd for a Friday night. Some from the Bots, some from the hospital, a big crowd from our place and the odd local guys from up the road.

Frank was getting a good send-off and even as we were listening to his story about an argument with a porter in Kildare Street another gang of people arrived in the door. He interrupted his story, bid them a welcome and ordered the drinks, and settled in to deliver the punchline. Most of us had heard the story before, but we waited in anticipation for the part of the story where himself and Paddy averted a national strike with a few well-chosen words.

By seven o'clock the crowd had grown considerably and eased off again as the family men who had come to pay their regards left for home and domesticity. A group of about fifteen of us had huddled into a corner and were swapping tales of incidents that had happened over the years. As one story would finish, another would be prompted and sometimes the story was told between three or four of us who were all there at the same time.

I thought about Marian and looked at my full pint in front of me. "I'll go after this one," I thought and headed to the loo. When I came back the conversation had turned to a history of Frank's life outside the service, and while he was being cagey, there were bits and pieces coming out that hadn't been heard before.

"Don't you own that flat where the guy was killed in Rathmines" suddenly one of the guys from the Post Room asked.

There was an awful silence for a second as everybody recoiled at the baldness of the question. Not only was it a sensitive subject, but there had been no pre-amble or introduction.

"Ranelagh," said Frank. "And yes, I do, for my sins." He looked into his pint, a far away and sad look in his eyes. "A house that has brought enough misery to me as any house could possibly do. Poor Carmel still has nightmares, waking up crying in the middle of the night about that little bastard who had himself slit in the flat."

We were all silent, a respectful hush had descended. The Post Boy, having got over the embarrassment at his ignorant question, was revelling in the fruits of his boldness, and hanging on every word out of Frank's mouth.

He was off. "A little tinker if ever I met one. Could look you in the eye and lie through his teeth. A full three months he was in that flat without paying a bit of rent. All I ever got out of him was a deposit and the promise of rent. He had poor Carmel's heart scalded with going down there and asking for the money. We had even gone so far as to get a solicitor. Oh, a nasty piece of work he was."

None of us dared to ask a question or interrupt the mood. We were all staring into our pints, with the occasional glance at the story-teller.

"And he went and ruined a good settee, the little bastard, with all that blood and gore," he laughed... And we all laughed, glad to be free of the seriousness of it.

"An awful thing to try and remove, that blood..." someone threw in.

"Clean it... we fucked the whole thing out, that and everything in the flat. Bad luck was all it was. Got a skip and turfed the whole lot into it.... And good riddance."

We all nodded vehemently.

"Who's for another one?" asked Sean, one of the older guys. "I'm off to the bar." And off he went with an order for 6 pints. The conversation drifted into other things and I saw Frank deep in conversation at the bar with Sean. I grabbed my coat and headed over to them.

"Frank, I have to be off. I'm meeting Marian over in Neary's."

We shook hands warmly. "You're a good lad, Ben. You'll do well."

"Keep in touch, Frank… and give my best to Carmel."

"I will Ben, I will."

We let the handshake go with a final squeeze and I clapped him on the shoulder.

"Enjoy it, Frank," I said and made my way through the pub to the door. I looked back and it was as if I was never there. Conversation had resumed and the hum of interaction continued.

I opened the door into the night air and ran across the road for a bus.

Chapter 10

"You knew the lad. Didn't you," whispered Frank to Ben, as they stood at the bar later in the evening. "He told me so when he was looking at the flat."

Ben looked at him enquiringly.

"He asked me was I paying tax on the rent. I was so taken aback by the question I told him where I worked, and that of course I was paying tax."

Ben looked at him and nodded.

"When he heard where I worked he said 'Oh, I know a guy in there, Ben Morris, a good friend of mine. Do you know him?'"

Ben shuddered at the description. His stomach churned.

"You did know him?" asked Frank, almost pleading.

"Aye, I knew him Frank. We went to school together, when we were very young. And if you'd asked me, I'd have told you he was a little shit."

"Yes, he said you went to school together. Sat beside each other. Were great friends.

"I thought… well, if he knows Ben, and is good friends with him, then he must be a good lad." He looked into the middle distance, a frown on his face.

"Now, I'm not blaming you, Ben. I should have asked you at the time. But I never thought. You know how it is."

Ben nodded, feeling sick.

"Did you meet up with him at all?"

"I didn't Frank. We fell out a long time ago and had nothing to say to each other."

The bells were ringing for last orders.

"But you were seen with him on the Saturday... in Slattery's..."

The bells were still ringing...

I woke up and reached for the alarm clock.

Chapter 11

I hate Christmas at the best of times. A big wind-up to a dreadful day that everybody heaves the most almighty sigh of relief when it's over. One of the great traditions we have to live with, and true to form, we all toe the party line and do the necessary.

The day before Christmas Eve is one of those almighty drinking sessions that starts with Kriskindle in the office. Everybody had been given a name of another office member and told to spend no more than a fiver on a present for this person. The names are picked out of a hat near the beginning of December and everyone has a month to find a vaguely embarrassing present for their individual victim.

I got Jeff, though I was under strict orders by the organisers not to breath a hint of who I'd got to anybody. It wasn't a difficult present to find. I had a choice of a personal organiser or a diary. He loathed both and seemed to find the concept of either completely beyond his comprehension.

The presents, wrapped in Christmas paper and left under the Weeping Fig tree that had been suitably festooned in the Christmas spirit, were individually handed out by Fidelma with loads of Ho Ho Ho's and general raucousness. All this was spurred on by a few bottles of gin and vodka, and the odd bottle of whiskey.

The party usually fades towards lunch hour when everybody heads over to The Tolka, has 'lunch' and stays there until mid afternoon... or however long they can stay drinking. Some have been known to stay until closing time. Others have been seen making their way up Glasnevin Road in no fit state to string a sentence together as early as two in the afternoon.

I stayed until three and then made my way into town to meet Marian. Her gang were meeting in The Long Hall and I'd said I'd get over there as early as I could. I still had two presents to get so I got off the bus in Parnell Square and walked through Moore Street to see what I could find in Henry Street and the small shops in Liffey Street.

It's funny how much easier it is to find those most difficult presents on the day before Christmas Eve with a few pints on you. I suppose the mixture of panic and alcohol take the edge off discernment and images of truly delighted faces are easier to imagine when looking at monumental candles then than they were when Christmas was a whole month away.

Laden with three candles and a big assortment of smellies in a very presentable cardboard box, I pushed my way through the crowd in The Long Hall. Marian was down the back. They had been able to commandeer a whole table and a gang of about fifteen of them were well into the 'drape ourselves around each other's shoulders and shout into faces' stage.

When she saw me making my way over to her, Marian's face lit up and she made a drunken lurch through the crowd and threw her arms around my neck, giving me a big sloppy kiss.

"My Ben," she slurred. "Everybody, Ben is here... say hello to Ben."

She whirled around and waved everybody around me. Hugs and kisses ensued and somehow my bags disappeared under chairs and I was presented with a pint of Guinness.

"Someone got one too many in the last round" Marian winked at me as she handed me the pint. "Did you get the last of your presents?"

We stayed for another three pints and then, wrapped around each other for support, staggered out of the pub at about eight o'clock weighed down with the last of her shopping and mine. Somehow, we made it back to my place without losing anything, and collecting a Chinese Take-Away along the route.

We woke up the following morning on the couch, the remnants of the Chinese on the coffee table in front of us.

"Morning" Marian mumbled from somewhere on my chest as she cuddled in closer. "What time is it?"

With difficulty I focused on my watch.

"Half past eight, time enough."

"What!" She sat up straight. "The bus is at eleven and I have to get home first.

Shit!"

I wasn't sure if the expletive was on account of the way she felt at the sudden movement or because of the rushing that she knew was ahead of her.

"Better get a move on then...." I mumbled, and received a dig in the ribs for my trouble.

The next half an hour was a chaotic mixture of elementary beautifying to get her from my flat to hers, a quick check of what she needed from my flat over the next five days, passionate (if half-hearted due to our current conditions) good-byes and complicated arrangements (at least they seemed complicated at that point) for calling over the holiday period and meeting up afterwards.

Once Marian had left it was into the shower and a thorough wash. A clean set of clothes later I began to load the table with all I wanted to bring with me to Limerford.

All the presents were identified and double-checked. A recurring nightmare was waking up on Christmas morning realising I had forgotten my Mother's Christmas present. Death was more appealing.

Enough clean clothes to do me that night and the following day, and enough clothes to do the next three days. Mum would have them clean by the time it came to wear them.

Money for the week and a few quid extra (no Cash Machines in Limerford) just in case.

Then it was a mad root to find hold-alls for it all.

By ten o'clock I was ready to go, and with a massive headache made my way into town for the bus, leaving a mess behind me that would grow mould in my absence.

No matter, I'd be so glad to get back to it by the time the holiday was over that the state of it wouldn't make any difference whatsoever.

I slept in the bus the whole way down and Mum was there at the bus-stop to meet me.

"Everybody else is here already," she greeted me. "Danny and Betty arrived last night and Jimmy arrived about an hour ago. Did you have a good journey?"

We talked ten to the dozen as we loaded the bags into the car and all the way back to the house. Betty was pregnant and Jimmy had split up with his girlfriend.

"Act surprised when you hear" Mum said, "But forewarned is forearmed. Just so you don't put your foot in it."

I didn't like to tell her that Jimmy's girlfriend was a bloke and that it was bound to break up since he had been a complete wanker and made Jimmy's life a misery for the three months they were seeing each other.

It was nice to hear Betty was expecting. They'd been married for five years and had been trying for a baby for over a year. After all the tests and trials nothing said they shouldn't have kids. It just wasn't happening. And now it had.

"Oh, and no doubt you heard about Bert McBride getting himself killed in Dublin." She announced just as we pulled into the drive.

It was a rhetorical question. As she said it she was pulling the key from the ignition and opening the car door.

"His mother must be turning in her grave. Though there's those who say it was no accident that she ended up in the river. Sort of ran in the family."

She gave me a wry look, as if to say that she knew she shouldn't be saying such things, but knew it was OK with me.

At that the front door flew open and Betty flew out to say hello.

"Where have you been? We thought the bus had crashed," she announced as she gave me a hug and took one of the bags out of the boot.

"Oh, leave them now," I said, taking it off her. "Not in your condition. Congratulations, by the way."

This led to another big hug and loads of gushing and laughing.

Eventually we all got inside and I threw my bags in my old bedroom. It was as it always was. Nothing had been moved, except of course to be dusted by my mother, who I'm sure cleaned it as she always had through my childhood. The bedclothes were clean and the heating had the room nice and comfy. Jimmy's bed on one side and mine on the other. The rows and arguments we had in that room.

I only had a small minute to absorb the feeling of being home in my room before I hurried down to the kitchen to take my place at the table for dinner. On my way in my father looked up from his paper, from where he sat beside the range.

"Hello son." He nodded over his glasses. "Did you have a nice trip down on the bus?"

"I did Dad, I slept most of the way."

"A good day yesterday then?"

We both laughed and he put away the paper and came to the table as my mother ladled soup into the bowls laid about the table.

The banter around the table was familiar and friendly as we worked our way through the 'snack' Mum had prepared. It was well past three o'clock before we were finished and Mum stacked the dishes to be washed. I went to give a hand but was shooed away.

"Surely you have people to be seeing in town. Get on with you and drop over to Frieda. She's been asking for you."

I took the opportunity being presented to me. The others were heading off to their own friends and the house would be quiet for the rest of the afternoon as Mum prepared the food for tomorrow.

I hitched a lift off Danny and Betty who were heading over towards Frieda's. She was playing with Cathal in the living room when I got there. I was only in the door when she had her coat on.

"I'm off down to Johnny's with Ben," she shouted to her mother as Cathal wandered into the kitchen to find new entertainment.

Her mother came out of the kitchen wiping her hands in a tea cloth.

"Ben, how are you? You're looking well," she said as she put the cloth over her shoulder and gave me a hug and a kiss on the cheek. "Happy Christmas to you. Is it dragging Frieda off to the pub you are?"

I looked suitably meek and humble and she laughed. "Go on the two of you. Have a good time. It's a break from this house she needs now. Don't get too drunk now."

"Well, what do you think of Bert McBride?" She asked me as soon as we were out on the road. "Wasn't that the thing now."

"It was surely," I said noncommittally.

"I never thought he'd get into that sort of trouble," she continued. "There's wild talk of all sorts of things going on. One story has it that he was dealing drugs. To be honest I wouldn't put it past him. Another story has it a lover's tiff. My own favourite is that he did it himself. When you look at how his sister did herself in, and then his mother. It all adds up."

"It was never proved that his sister did herself in. Nor his mother for that matter," I countered, though why I bothered I couldn't figure.

"True. But it's odd all the same." She was linking me as we walked down the road and it felt good to be with her again. We'd gotten to a point where we were like brother and sister and felt comfortable with each other without feeling awkward with intimacies.

"I guess that makes Cathal an orphan so," she giggled. It was obvious there had been no love lost between Bert and Frieda over the four years since Cathal was born. Bert's death, under whatever circumstances, mattered less to her than a change in the weather.

"Did you go to the funeral?" I asked. Again, I had no idea why I bothered. I really didn't want to know and would have preferred if the conversation weren't happening. On the other hand, I didn't want it to look suspicious. It wasn't as if I didn't know the guy and it was a juicy bit of gossip. It would have looked more than odd if I avoided the subject like I would have preferred to.

"I did," she said. "And it was a pretty quiet occasion. There's not many of his family left and he didn't have many friends left in the town. If there was thirty people at the funeral, that was it. I went with me Ma and Cathal. It would have been a bit obscene not to have brought Cathal to his own father's funeral" she finished almost defensively.

"Oh, it would. No matter what, he was his father," I agreed.

"It was sort of sad at the grave-yard." she went on. "There weren't many people around the grave. A couple of his uncles came over from Mullingar with their wives, but other than that and us there was nobody else.

"After the prayers were over, we all just went our different ways.

"Sad really. For all the little shit that he was you would have wanted more for him than that."

I found myself agreeing with her. It was a sad sort of a send off.

We walked in silence for a few minutes.

"Did you hear that Betty is pregnant?" I asked, more to lighten the mood than to pass on the story.

"Oh, that's great. They've been trying for a bit haven't they," she enthused as we got to Johnnys and walked into the warmth of the pub.

It was pretty full. All sorts of people home for the Christmas and a right lively atmosphere.

"What'll you have?" I asked as I headed over to the bar and Frieda waved to a group of our school friends in the corner.

"Bacardi and Coke," she threw over her shoulder as she waded in their direction.

****

It took him an age to get to the bar, talking to people every step of the way.

"A pint of Guinness and a Bacardi and Coke."

Then it moved in like a cold wind from the door. People were looking at him a little differently. He could almost see it passing him by from one side of the room to the other. One minute people were talking to him about Christmas, Santa Claus, booze ups and presents and then, as if they were waiting for him to take off his coat, they were moving up to him and listening to what he was saying in an eerie sort of way.

It wasn't the same 'chat away because it's Christmas' sort of listening. It was a 'hang on his every word because it could mean something' type of listening. It was as if he had a secret they knew about but hadn't yet been told and wanted to hear it from the horse's mouth.

And suddenly they had realised that he had arrived. When he came in first they were caught unawares and hadn't noticed he was there. But then somebody clicked and in an instant the realisation was moving around the room, almost visible in the change in people's movement. One minute it was on one side of him and like a wave it moved over him and was throughout the whole room... the whole pub.

Just as he passed the tenner to the barman he could feel it passing over the bar. It was as if in the split second between the note being in his hand and in the barman's hand the wave had crossed the counter and when he was getting his change it was from a different man.

"Take care Ben." As if in slow motion, he winked and held on to the money for that microsecond longer than was necessary. "Take care," and he was gone, handing out two pints to the next punter.

It didn't take so long to get back to Frieda.

"Good man. Maura here was just telling me about her new car. A Punto. She can't get over the difference in being able to get around."

"I can't get over the difference. The independence. The power. 'Mum, would you like a lift into town?', 'Freddy, I'll give you a lift into the pub if you wash my new car tomorrow.'"

They all laughed because it was impossible to get her brother Freddy to scratch himself unless it has a direct benefit to himself.

"Here, what's this I hear about yourself?" Maura suddenly asked, as if it had only just popped into her mind.

"What's that?"

"You know.... You and Bert McBride?"

He hoped he managed to look puzzled as his stomach clenched and his face went bright red. "It's a hot pub," he thought furiously. "I don't LOOK red."

"Bert McBride? What about him?"

"Stabbed in his living room. Dead as a door nail."

"Ease up there Maura," said Frieda. "The father of my child. A bit of respect there." But they could see she wasn't upset, just taking the mickey.

Ben was frantic inside, looking from one to the other. What were they getting at?

"Oh, Ben, you're at home now. What DID happen? Tell us... Do."

The two eager faces were looking at him expectantly, but they weren't the only ones watching him. There was a wider circle of faces, curious ears, earwigging into the conversation.

"I've no idea what you mean," he said, trying to pass over the conversation. "What have you been hearing?"

He turned to Frieda for support, but she was looking at him with a look of undisguised injury. She was looking as if he was deliberately not playing along and hiding something from her. Didn't she deserve more than this pretense of innocence.

"Come on Ben. It's not as if it's not obvious. You hated him as long as you've known him. Don't try and pretend you didn't do it. Everybody knows."

"What? What do you mean?" He couldn't believe what he was hearing. Frieda gave no indication on the way down that she had any idea.

"Come on Ben, do tell." encouraged Maura. "Was there a fight?"

His head reeled. How could he say it was protecting Frieda's honour he was? It'd sound so trite. It'd drag up a past he thought he had put nicely to sleep. Frieda didn't need to hear what Bert had been saying about her.

Anyway, what was he thinking about? They COULDN'T know. Where were they coming from?

Suddenly there was a hand on his shoulder. Jimmy was whispering in his ear. "Ben, I need to talk to you. Have you a minute?"

"Sure, sure," he grabbed the opportunity. "I'll be back in a minute" he said over his shoulder as they moved towards the door and found a quiet spot beside the cigarette machine.

"Ben, it's out. People know."

Shook, Ben looked at Jimmy like a rabbit caught in the headlights.

"Frank Wilson just told me he knew I was gay. What the fuck do I do? It'll be around the whole town in no time at all."

"Wha?" said Ben, stupidly. "Frank Wilson... Gay?"

"Yes, gay. He said he knew I was gay. Holy mother of God. What'll I do?"

"What do you mean, what'll you do? How does he know? Where did he find out?"

"He said he saw me in The George, you know, the gay pub. So he put two and two together. So he knows."

"Tell me Jimmy. What was he doing in The George? Did you ask yourself that one?"

Jimmy looked gobsmacked. "You mean?"

"It's a possibility. How did he say it to you? Was it a threat, or a question? Maybe he IS gay. And if that's the case then he's hardly going to have THAT spread about the town. Would you calm down and not be panicking."

"You know, you might be right Ben. He might be...

"Now that you say it, I think he was saying it to test the waters...

"You could be right." He looked much relieved.

"Jimmy... how did you leave it with him? Did you deny it or what?"

"I didn't say anything. Just after he said it Billy Adams pushed his way into the conversation and I went to go to the jax. And here I am talking to you...

"God, Ben. Thanks a million. I never thought of that one. Wow! Frank Wilson gay. Holy God."

"Take it easy Jimmy, he might not be. But if he was in The George then he's at least not a homophobe so it's not something to be panicking about. Take it easy."

"OK, OK. Thanks Ben. You're a star. See you later."

"If only it was always that simple," thought Ben, as he headed back to Frieda. On the way back he wondered if he should go back at all, or if he should just make a run for it.

"Better face the music now," he thought. "I couldn't spend the night wondering what they DO know."

But he never got as far as Frieda. On the way he was stopped by Maura's brother, Freddy.

"Fair dues Bud," he said clapping him on the shoulder. "Nice one."

People were looking at him now. A few people were smiling at him, almost congratulatory, but others were avoiding his eyes.

He pretended not to hear what Freddy had said, and kept walking towards Frieda. But again he was stopped.

"Is it true what they say Ben? That you're the man?"

"I'm not so sure I know what you mean." He was hassled now. He could see Frieda behind them now, looking at him. She was moving towards him.

He signalled to her as if they were being interrupted and he had to go... but a hand grabbed him from behind, stopped him moving forward...

He fought to move forward...

I woke up with Jimmy shaking my arm. I was fighting to get away from him.

"Are you all right Ben? What were you dreaming? Are you awake now?"

There was concern in his voice. I must have been making quite a racket. His hand was still on my shoulder, but it was placating now; he was trying to soothe me.

"That must've been some dream boy. You nearly had the whole town awake. Are you all right now? Do you want a cup of tea?"

I looked into his worried face and saw the empathy coming out to me.

"No. No. I'm grand. It was just a nightmare. I'll be fine now.

"Thanks.

"Go back to bed now. Thanks. I'll be grand."

He went back to his bed and soon I could hear him asleep again. But it was a while before I got back to sleep.

****

Jimmy was gone and the light streaming in the window when I awoke the following morning. I could hear Mum shouting downstairs that breakfast was nearly ready.

"You had a good time last night in town?" asked my father as I settled myself at the breakfast table.

"I did. I did. There was such a crowd in the pub. Just about everybody is home. How did you get on Jimmy?"

His mouth full of toast Jimmy expressed great enthusiasm for last night, waving his arms about and nodding furiously. He gulped the mouthful down.

"What a crowd. I'd say just about everybody I grew up with was there somewhere."

"All except Bert McBride," said Betty facetiously.

"Funny enough, there was no mention of him at all. It was as if he'd never existed at all."

"Mmm that's true. I didn't hear a mention of him at all."

"No, me neither. I guess people don't want to be bothered with that sort of sadness at Christmas."

It was then that I remembered that the only person who had mentioned it had been Frieda, and that was on the way to the pub. I guess people didn't want to be remembering it.

"Sad, all the same."

"Anybody for more toast?" Asked my mother, obviously trying to change the subject. Life was too short for that sort of talk on a Christmas morning. "Are we opening the presents before or after Mass?"

"Oh, we have to do it before Mass. I need to wear what Danny bought me."

"No. No. After Mass. We always do it after Mass," said Jimmy.

All eyes looked at Mum to adjudicate.

"We can all open ONE present before Mass and the rest can wait until afterwards," she decreed. There was a rush for the sitting room as we all went to pick the grandest looking one for opening now.

It was just as well we did because Betty would have looked funny going to Mass without the Calvin Klein jeans Danny had bought her. The only other pair she had with her were only fit for a dig out in the garden.

Not the way to go to Mass of a Christmas morning.

****

It was a jolly sort of day and by three in the afternoon we were all stretched out in the Living Room glad to have nothing more exciting ahead of us but a few old movies.

At five o'clock Marian rang me and we spent a half an hour on the phone. That didn't go without comment when I got back for the end of the film.

"That sounds serious," said Danny. "You were nearly out there an hour."

"A half an hour," I retorted. "Don't exaggerate."

"Who's counting? Long enough to be serious. What are your intentions, young man?"

"Oh, leave him alone," said my mother, "You had your day without that sort of ragging."

"Well as it may be, but I was never the afternoon on the phone."

"Well as it may be, I only lived down the road," said Betty. "How is she getting on, Ben?"

"Ah, she had a grand day. They're doing the same as we are, stretched out in front of the TV."

"What did you get her?"

"A dose of jewelry, all matching. She picked it herself. Earrings, necklace, and watch. Cost a fortune."

"Ah, the wristwatch. Secret engagement." said Danny, not prepared to let it go.

"Anyone for sandwiches?" asked my mother before I had time to respond. "C'mon Betty. Giv's a hand to put something together."

"Now see what you done," said Betty, digging Danny in the ribs as she got up. "Ye just can't shut it. Can ye?"

We all laughed and there was a general movement as nature's calls were answered and Dad went out to the yard to have a smoke. I went out with him, just for a bit of fresh air.

"You didn't sleep too well last night son? Is everything all right?" he asked as we leaned against the back wall and looked out over the fields. It was dark, but it was a nice evening, dry and not too cold.

"Ah, a bit of a nightmare Dad. I can't even remember it now. Something I drank maybe."

"Maybe. Or something on your mind?"

He waited.

I waited.

He took another drag of his cigarette.

"Not a bad evening," he said, to keep the conversation going.

"Aye, for the time of year, it's great."

I waited.

He waited.

"It comes to us all eventually," he said softly.

"What's that?" I asked.

"Death. It's just a little bit of a shock when it's someone our own age."

"Ah..." I said, realising where he was going.
"Right."

"It doesn't make it any easier for us, but it's a part of growing up. Learning to live with it."

I looked at him, and he looked at me... and for a fleeting moment I thought he was saying something else to me. As if he knew...

"Chin up son, I guess we just have to live with it," he said as he put his arm around my shoulder and led me back into the house. "We'd better do some damage to these sandwiches or your Mother'll have words to say."

Chapter 12

It seemed like no time at all before I was loading my bags back in the car and Mum was dropping me up to the bus.

"Have you everything with you Ben?" she asked as we were driving down to the Main Street.

"I have Mum. And sure, anything I don't have I can collect the next time I'm down."

"Are you all right, Ben?" she asked suddenly. "Is there anything wrong?"

"No, Mum. Why do you ask that?"

"Well, you just seemed a little bit distracted a few times over the time. There's something on your mind.

"Your father thinks so too," she added, as if to lend weight.

"No, Mum. I'm OK. There's nothing to be worried about."

We pulled in beside the line of people opposite Murphy's Drapers.

"Well, you know Ben that we're always here for you." She turned and looked at me straight. "No matter what." She reached out and took my hand in hers. "Remember, no matter what, Ben. No matter what."

There were a hint of tears in my eyes. "I know Mum. Thanks."

We sat looking at each other for a second and then she shrugged. "Once you know Ben. Let's get these bags out of the boot and have you off."

We unloaded the boot and I gave her a hug before she got back in the car.

"No matter what Ben," she whispered in my ear and was gone into the car.

I waved her away down the road, and again when she passed back up the road towards home.

"Indeed," I thought to myself, "no matter what. Hopefully Mum, there won't be a matter what."

I stared after the car and waited for the bus. I knew everybody there at the queue, but none of them as much as I'd want to talk to them. When the bus came, I was happy to find a seat down the back on my own. I threw my bags on the seat beside me in case anybody felt they might want to talk to me and stuck my head facing the window and watched the side of the road the whole way up to Dublin.

"No matter what."

"We've got to live with it."

It was over two months now. I guess I was living with it. But it was only a matter of time before they caught up with me. Nobody gets away with murder. They were sure to put it all together eventually. And then I was for the chop. Then the 'matter what' would be out on the table.

The unmentionable ran through my mind. Mum's face. Dad's look. The feeling of shame they'd both have to live with. Their son a murderer.

That cold sweat crept over me and swamped my mind.

The shame. Having to face everyone as a murderer. Sweat covered my face. I felt I was going to be sick.

"Shit. It hasn't happened yet. Don't get yourself in a heap over wild imaginings. They have no proof. Nobody saw you. You left no evidence... no fingerprints... nothing to say you were even at the scene."

I kept telling myself, over and over.

But I didn't believe it.

I was guilty as hell, and it was only a matter of time.

As we approached the centre of Dublin I decided to enjoy my last days of freedom. Devil take it all. What could I do about it now?

Nothing.

"Live with it."

Marian was waiting in Mulligans for me. She'd gotten an earlier bus and was in town a half an hour earlier than me.

"You look like you could do with a pint," she said as I pushed my way in the door with my bags. "Sort yourself out there while I get you one."

"Was it a bad bus journey?" she asked when she got back. "You look a bit rough."

"Maybe I'm coming down with something," I replied. "I've not been sleeping well. Maybe I've got a dose of 'flu or something."

"Oh, you poor lad. What sort of a Christmas was it for you? Good, eh?"

"Not bad. Not bad at all." I sipped my pint and looked at her. I had missed her. More than I had thought.

"And what about you? A good time?"

She nodded.

"What was the crack?"

That was all she needed.

She launched into a reverie about how her brother had got turfed out twice from the garage, and each time got back in again after his father went to talk to MickeyJoe and talked him around. Each time her father had to go then to Alan and give him a pep talk about the trials and tribulations of working life, about discipline and about earning the few bob at the end of the week.

By all accounts some of the fundamentals like turning up every day, listening to what he's being asked to do and doing that - instead of what he thinks would be more fun doing - were going straight over his head. Marian herself had a deep and meaningful chat with him at some stage over the weekend and he's beginning to understand the concept of work.

To be honest he always seems a bit of a gobshite to me, but it's more than my life is worth to ever pretend this to Marian. She only sees her little brother, and since he's a Howard - he's perfect. Maybe not everybody's idea of perfect, but it's all subjective, or objective, or whatever it is, and not to be brought up on New Year's Eve when you haven't seen your girlfriend for a whole week.

I nodded like the nodding dog in the back of her father's car and she moved on to her mother's Christmas Dinner and the scandal of the woman next door who had stolen - stolen no less - her Christmas turkey from the local butchers. It all got a little complicated when the detail was exposed to the cold light of day, but it seemed to me that the woman had picked up the wrong end of the stick from a rather uncommunicative butcher and now her name was mud from one end of the town to the other. Somehow the story went on then to describe the butcher's sexual adventures with a variety of housewives and my nasty mind sloped off to thinking this might be a case of the scorned butcher's revenge.

But again, I wasn't so sure of my facts that I put forward the theory.

In fact, the only thing that slowed Marian down for a moment was the sight of the bottom of her glass and I was dispatched for a set of refills while she went off to the loo.

I went up to the bar and hailed the barman, signalling that I wanted two more pints. He waved from where he was and set about pulling them. I stood with an elbow at the bar and looked around, casting a quick glance at the bags to see there was no-one running off with my newly washed clothes and my Christmas loot, not to mention Marian's collection of bags.

Security confirmed, I looked around the pub at the bentwood chairs, the old rickety tables, the wooden floorboards, the cream plaster walls and wondered had it changed at all in a hundred years. You could be at any point in time over the past hundred years, with only the clothes giving some indication of the age we're living in.

Suddenly from my left I heard two guys talking behind the partition along the bar.

"'T'was a messy affair by all accounts. If the story Paddy was telling me is even half true then he was properly carved up."

"Is that so now? And was there any sign of a struggle, or was it a quick one?"

"A dirty one, I believe. Must've been quite a fight. The furniture was all over the place and the floor covered in blood. Paddy thinks it was a gang went in and took care of him."

There was a silence for a bit.

"Drugs?"

"To be sure. Isn't that the reason for all the trouble in this city."

"Two pints of Guinness." The barman was back with my pints.

"G'd Man. Thanks a million." I passed him the money and was just getting back to the table when Marian returned.

"What do you women be doing in there for that length of time? I ask you?"

She gave me a withering look and took a sip from her fresh pint.

"More than you'd be wanting to know."

I beat a hasty retreat. Time of the month was NOT a conversation I wanted to get into.

"Have you any plans for us tonight or should I give a few people a ring and see what's happening?" I asked.

"I was talking to Mary. She wants us all to meet up in McSorley's and there is a chance of a party in their place."

My heart dropped to the pit of my stomach. Not again... please. Not again.

"On the other hand, there is a party with the crowd from work and Moira is trying to push that. That crowd is meeting up in The Stag's Head and everybody is going on then to Mick McMenamin's flat in Temple Bar."

"Now that sounds like a bit of crack," I answered... maybe too quickly.

"But you can't stand Mick McMenamin."

"I'm sure there'll be more than the two of us at the party. I don't have to do more than say hello, do I?"

She was still a little suspicious.

"I've never been to a flat in Temple Bar. I'd say they are pretty cool inside... and if you say that to that cretin Mick McMenamin I'll have your guts for garters."

We both laughed.

"So, you think we should swing with Moira."

I nodded. "Mmmm, I do. It'll be a nice change to get into town. McSorley's is grand, but we were there just before Christmas and the centre of town could be a bit of fun. We might even get up to Christ Church for the Bells at Midnight."

"For all that's worth. I believe that can be an over-rated event. Some stories I've heard has it that it's a bit of a drunken affair, with lots of loud mouth boyos just raring for a fight."

"We should fit in so," I joked, and got a thump on the shoulder.

"Hang on and I'll ring Mary and see what the latest story is." Then she looked around. "Maybe I'd better go outside and ring. I'll be back in a minute."

It was well more than a minute she was gone and I looked over at the two guys who had been talking at the other side of the partition. They were both in their fifties and probably worked in the refurbishment business. Not rough men, but had a look about them that said hard work and lots of it. Both of them had fine big beer bellies and frames that carried them comfortably. They were wearing big woolly jumpers and peaked caps and looked as if they had being doing a bit of work that very morning. Their formless trousers had the dust of a few days' work on them and their boots had only vague memories of what shoe polish could do for them.

They were still deep in that desultory conversation and wouldn't have wandered far from Paddy's revelations on the murder. I wasn't sure they were talking about the Ranelagh murder, but I suspected they might have been. My guess was that Paddy was the guy who had gutted the flat afterwards and had cleaned the place out for Frank. Either that or he was a friend of the guy who did.

As usual the story had been embellished a bit along the way.

All the same, it was a small world. You can never be sure of who you're talking to, or who might be listening.

"It's all sorted." I looked up, startled.

"Wha?"

"McSorley's...." She waited for my reaction.

"... and then into town to the Stag's Head." She smiled and sat herself back down into her seat.

"Moira figures that Temple Bar is THE place to spend New Year's Eve, so we're heading in there.

"On the other hand, The Stag's Head will be packed so we'll meet up in McSorley's at nine o'clock and have a couple there. Then at about ten o'clock Mary's fella, Seamus, will come and collect us - he's coming up from Cork and won't be around until then - and drive us all into his flat near Christ Church. He'll drop us off at the bottom of Dame Street and by the time he's parked the car we'll have a pint and a short ready for him, poor cratur trying to catch up with the rest of us."

It was all said in one stream, with hardly a break for breath. Then she took a swig of her pint and looked at me.

"How's that for a plan?" she asked.

"Sounds fine to me... " I looked settled but dubious.

"But...."

"There's many a slip between the cup and the lip. Too many arrangements in the one plan and there's bound to be a hitch somewhere."

"Misery guts," she retorted and I smiled. "But it'll be all great fun because no matter where we end up I'll have you to look at. And isn't that heaven itself."

She smiled coyly. "You say the nicest of things Mr. Morris."

"C'mon," I said. "Let's go and get this gear home and make some inroads to getting to the first stage of the plan."

"Aye," she said. "Washed. I could do with a good scrub down after that bus journey."

"Your wish is my command. Hand me the brush and let me get scrubbing."

We collected up our bags, took the final swig from our glasses, banged our way out the half doors of the pub and fell out into the bright daylight of the street.

"Bus or taxi?"

"Let's see if we can pick up a taxi?" she said, and we walked around to the quays to see if we could hail a taxi down.

****

The plan was to drop Marian off at her flat and let her get in, unpack her bags, get washed up and come over to my place for a bit to eat before we headed down to McSorley's.

When I got back to my place the smell of mouldy Chinese met me at the front door. It was as if there was a dead body somewhere in the house. For the first time in my life, I could forgive Mrs. Blake if she met me on the stairs and gave me a roasting. It was disgusting.

Huh! See what living at home for a few days does to your stamina. No sense of resilience for the harsher side of life.

I grinned to myself as I opened the door of the flat.

Then the full blast of the smell hit me. Stamina or no, I had to open a window.

I dropped my bags by the door and opened all the windows, rooting in the press for some air freshener. With an old tee shirt over my face, I gathered together the mess on the coffee table and brought it over to the bin.

That was worse.

I had left the heater on over the whole of Christmas and the room was a breeding ground for any sort of fungi possible. I'm sure in the time I'd been away I had invented a whole new league of varieties of fungus.

I rooted out a black plastic sack and put the bin, the Chinese, the litter on the floor and the contents of an ashtray (That must have been there for a while... neither of us smoke anymore.) inside. With as much speed as possible I knotted the top, sealing the smell inside. Then I went outside with the bag and left it in the refuse area with all the other bins.

I was just back inside the house when I heard the door into the flat above slam shut.

"Shit!" I had left my keys in my coat, on the sofa upstairs. As if hurrying would make a difference, I rushed up the stairs and tried the door.

Yes. I was locked out.

I had a choice. Wait for Marian to come over, or try and get in. At least I had all the windows open.

An hour later and my trousers nicely muddied from climbing a tree, jumping onto the outhouse roof, scrambling across the ledge - firmly gripping the toilet pipe from upstairs for balance - onto the window sill, I landed into the 'kitchen' and gave a whoop of sheer achievement.

I would not make a cat-burglar.

Just as I had finished congratulating myself the doorbell rang. Careful to make sure I had the keys this time I went downstairs and opened the front door, expecting it to be Marian.

Two Gardaí stood at the door. My mind went into overload. I immediately thought the worst.

"We were told that a man was seen trying to make entry into this house via a back, first floor window. Would you know anything about that?"

My relief was palpable.

"Yes, that was me."

His look said it all. I was to be marched away there and then and charged with breaking and entry.

Hurriedly I continued. "I locked myself out when I went to leave the bins out. There was a horrible smell in the flat when I got back after the Christmas."

They looked at me with that condescending way only Gardaí (and Marian) can muster.

"So, I had to get back in by the back window."

"Do you have any form of identification?"

"Mmmm, Yes... I do... upstairs...." and we all heard the door bang shut again.

"And this time I have a key."

We were just about to go up the stairs when Mrs. Blake's door swung open.

"Ben Morris, if you don't stop banging that goddamn door upstairs I'll call the fucken peelers on you."

She had it said and was herself just into the hall before she saw the three of us on the stairs.

"There'll be no need for that Ma'am. We're already here," said the Garda nearest her. "Can you confirm that this man is the rightful inhabitant of the flat upstairs."

Completely unsettled she gaped for a minute, took a look at me and said "Yes, Officer, That's him." and I'm not sure it wasn't said in the same way as she would if she were identifying the culprit in a line-up.

"Well, we'll not be bothering you any more Mr. Morris," he said and retraced his steps to the front door. "Make sure you keep your keys with you in future.

"Indeed Officer," I said as I followed them out. "Happy New Year and thanks for answering the call."

The walked down the path and closed the gate after them. From the look of them I don't know whether they thought I was a complete goon or pitied me having to live upstairs from Mrs. Blake.

"And Happy New Year to you too Mrs. Blake," I said as I closed the front door and bounded up the stairs.

Marian would be over any minute now and here I was with nothing but a story for her.

Albeit a pretty good one.

I had only closed the windows when the doorbell rang again. This time it was Marian and I had left the lock on the snib when I went down to answer it.

"Are you ready to go yet?" she loped into the house. "Moira was just on the phone. We're meeting earlier in McSorley's. Apparently, Seamus is arriving earlier and we have to be there at half past eight."

"Sorry luv, no can do. You'll never believe what happened."

We opened the door into the flat.

"What a pong!" she giggled. "That Chinese. You never cleaned it up before you left... did you?"

"No, and wait 'til I tell you.... Be a dear there and put on the kettle while I have a shower."

As I threw my bags into the bedroom and started undressing for a shower, I told her the story and took the mug of tea she'd made into the bathroom with me. She thought the whole thing hilarious and I could see her mind padding out the edges for telling in the pub that night.

She made herself busy with the air freshener and began to tidy the place up as I stepped into the shower. When I re-emerged, shaved and washed, she was sitting watching some old film on the TV.

"I would have loved to see that ol' bats face when she realised there were two cops on the stairs with you. "There'll be no need for that Ma'am. We're already here."" she mimicked the copper, hugging herself with glee. "What a blinder!"

We chatted through the wall as she went over the details again and again.

"And how did you get onto the roof of the outhouse?"

"And was it scary on the ledge?"

"Imagine the pipe had of come away in your hands. All that jax water all over you."

"Please Marian, it was bad enough as it was without THAT." I laughed. I was dressed now and ready to eat.

"What will we do for food?"

She looked at me as if I had just farted. "Food?"

"Yup, that stuff you put in your mouth. If I don't have some soon then I'll fade away long before the new year."

"I never thought about it," she said. "Will McDonald's in Ranelagh be open?"

"I guess we'd better have a look and see. There's nothing in this house to eat... except that pudding and cake my mother gave me."

****

We arrived into McSorley's just before nine with a feed of McDonald's inside of us.

"Line up the pints," I said. "I'm dying of thirst."

"Let me see where the gang are and you go and get them in."

I headed to the bar and before I even got the order in she was standing beside me pulling my coat.

"They're down the back, in the middle. Ye know, just beside the bar."

I knew where she was talking about and nodded.

"Seems there may be a problem with Mary. She doesn't seem the best."

I raised my eyebrows. "Yea?"

"Something to do with Mark, I think. There's no sign of him."

"Ah!"

I paid for the drinks and handed her a pint, following her around to where the others were.

Mary WAS looking a little peaky.

"Happy New Year all," I said as we arrived and they all pushed up to let us into the circle.

There was a general murmur of happy returns and the conversation went back to what they were discussing before the interruption.

"On New Year's Eve of all nights. And where do you think he got to?" Moira was all concern.

"Don't you know where he got to? He got drunk, the little bollix!" Mary retorted. "Doesn't he always get drunk. And it's New Year's Eve. He's probably been drinking since he left this morning."

"But he said he'd meet you at seven o'clock."

"In the flat," agreed Mary forlornly. "And I waited until eight, and then half past eight." Her eyes were welling up in tears and I pitied the guy when eventually he did turn up. "And he's got his mobile phone turned off so I can't find out where he is."

"Oh, it's probably not turned off deliberately," Seamus rushed to save a moment. "He probably left it behind him or forgot to turn it on."

Mary looked at him with a mixture of 'Thanks for making the effort but really I'd rather you didn't bother' and 'Who do you think you're codding? The little bollix is away without a free pass and don't you - member of the male establishment - try to cover up from him'. I wasn't sure which it was meant to be, but I determined there and then to keep my nose firmly out of this one.

However, Marian was just catching up with the flow of things. "When did you last hear from him?" she asked.

Mary burst into tears. "He went out this morning to get a newspaper."

Moira had to continue the story. "He stayed over last night because they missed the last bus home and it was shorter to get to Ranelagh than to try and get out to Leixlip...."

Seamus and myself exchanged glances. Yea, right!

"Then when we woke up this morning, we made a bite to eat and started making all the arrangements for tonight. He began to get a bit fidgety and said he would go out and get a newspaper. On his way out the door he shouted that if he wasn't back immediately that he's see us there in the flat at seven. We thought it a bit strange but passed it off as being Mark."

"And you haven't seen or heard from him since?" asked Marian.

"Not a word," said Mary.

"Bollix!" said Marian.

I was just about to say that if he was in the flat for the arrangements then he knew where to get us, but I thought better of keeping my mouth shut. As it was, I was beaten to the post by Seamus.

"Will we head down to The Stag's Head so I can leave the car in the flat?" he asked, completely unaware of what reaction that might provoke. As it was, he got off lightly.

"Well, we can't stay here for the night in the hope he might turn up," said Marian as reasonably as she could, with a touch of pleading in her voice.

"And he knows we were heading for The Stag's Head," added Moira, with the same hint of pleading.

"Sure, he's probably down there before us," said Seamus, putting his big size nines into it and squishing them about a bit. Mary burst into tears again.

However, the start had been made and we collected our coats and led a tearful Mary out to the car.

I don't know what they said to her on the way around to the car, Seamus and myself held back a little and let them walk ahead, but when we got there she had perked up a bit and was wiping her nose in a tissue, sitting in the back seat between Marian and I as we pulled out into Ranelagh village.

Seamus dropped us out at the bottom of George's Street and we took the lane into The Stag's Head. The place was crowded and I was dispatched up to get drinks while the ladies found Mick McMenamin and his party and a good place to stand nearby.

I guess we were all keeping our eye out for Mark, but it was no surprise when I arrived back to the girls and there was still no sign of him. Seamus arrived back at about the same time as me (I had his Guinness on for him, with a short of whiskey.) and we all huddled into the corner just inside the door of the snug.

Mercifully Mick Mc kept himself over the far side of the snug, caught in behind a table with a crowd of people. If I didn't concentrate on the conversation beside me I could still hear his high pitched voice across the room.

"But Muriel, of course we have some back at the apartment. What sort of a party would it be without some of that?"

I could only imagine what 'that' was, but I supposed it wasn't beer, and was more likely accompanied by loads of water. It takes all sorts to make a world.

Painfully, the conversation on this side of the room was not much better. Mary was still managing to get mileage out of her errant boyfriend. Why didn't she just ditch him and take up with someone else?

"Did you go home for Christmas?" Seamus was just as bored with it as I was.

"I did. Came back up this morning. When did you head down to Cork yourself?

"On the Tuesday. I'd a few days coming to me and my father is not well so I went down to do a bit of work on the farm. Getting things ready, you know." I didn't, being a townie, but I nodded sagely.

"Is there only yourself then? No brothers or sisters?"

"Not a bit of it. There are seven of us. Three of us in England, two in Dublin, and the last two stayed at home to mind the farm."

I nodded.

"But it's good to lend a hand now and then. Keep the finger in, as they say."

Marian nudged me and whispered in my ear. "Mary looks like she'll keep this up all night. I'm really sorry."

"Sorry nothing. Where else would I be but here with you. Do you think some drink might help?"

Just then, through the gap in the bar through to the main part I spotted Mark making his way through the crowd.

"Well, will you look what the cat dragged in," I muttered. "Stand back and hold your popcorn tight. This could be some performance."

Marian looked at me funny and then followed the line of my vision. "Holy Mother of God, Moira. Will ye look."

Moira turned her head, let out a whoop, and gave Mary an unmerciful bang on the shoulder. "Mary, he's here. He's here. Dry your eyes before he gets here. Don't let him see you were crying."

"Ahhh... I'm off to the loo. Marian, come on. Come with me. Moira. Tell him I'm in the loo."

Mark opened the door of the back hallway only to catch sight of the two of them scurrying down the stairs to the loo. The door was open to the snug, so he saw us all standing there and waved as if he hadn't a care in the world.

"Ah, found you at last. I've been looking all over for you. Was that Mary I saw dashing off to the loo?"

"It was Mark," said Seamus. "Will you have a pint?"

"And I'd be getting me story straight as to why you weren't in the flat at seven o'clock," finished Moira.

"I will Seamus," he said, accepting the offer and looking at Moira with a puzzled look on his face.

"What are you talking about Moira? Story straight? Seven o'clock. There was no mention of all that. What are you on about girl?"

Either he was a bloody good actor or as thick as two short planks, but he sure had me fooled. So long as he could hold it out until Mary came back.

Moira pointed out that he's left the flat that morning saying he'd be back at seven, and he hadn't been seen since.

He was good, I had to give him that. He didn't even try to deny it.

"Did I say that? Fuck me. I don't remember at all. I thought it was all wide open. A bus passed just as I was coming up to the shop so I hopped on and went into town. When I got home I fell asleep on the couch and only woke up an hour ago."

"Well, I'd come up with something better than that if I were you," said Moira, as Mary appeared back in the door from the loo.

"Where were you, you little bollix?" At least she was consistent. What she said behind his back she said to his face. "Seven o'clock. You said you'd be back at seven o'clock."

We all looked on, torn between wishing we weren't there, and thanking God it wasn't us.

"Mary, I'm really sorry. Moira's just told me. I got it all wrong. I didn't think we'd made arrangements. I'm really sorry."

I had to hand it to him. It wasn't so much what he said, it was the way he said it. And the little errant boy chastised look that oozed from his every pore was enough to melt the hardest heart. If he could bottle it, he'd be a millionaire.

Mary wasn't the hardest heart, and you could see her visibly weaken.

"Pints for the boys," said Seamus. "And something more dainty for the ladies," he said passing through the drinks... pints all of them.

But he was a clever man. The distraction took the heat off Mark and while the focus was away from him I nudged Marian and asked "Should we get some take-away for this party or is it all in hand with Mick McMen?"

This, of course was a red rag to a bull. Moira and Mick Mc used to be an item years ago and he was as tight as a nun's knickers when it came to spending money on other people. He always made it sound as if he was spending all around him on drinks, drugs and wild wild women, but when the push came to the shove, he was as mean as they come.

"Drink! Laid on!" scoffed Moira. "You must be joking. You'd sooner get... Mark to turn up when he's supposed to."

We all laughed, Mary included.

After that it was a grand night. We stayed in the Stag's Head until the New Year was rung in and at about half past midnight the barmen were anxious to get us out. Mick McMenamin was gone ahead of us, but Moira knew the way there, so we all bundled ourselves around to the flat and arrived on a scene already full of the joys of the season.

I didn't see much of Marian after that. She disappeared into the kitchen with Moira and I stood chatting to Seamus for a while. Eventually Mary and Mark showed up, each grinning from ear to ear and Mark sauntered over to the two of us. Before long the group got bigger and smaller and bigger again. I ended up standing at the window, just beside the balcony with this little fellow from Limerick who was big into defending the name of his home city.

"Sure, there's more stabbing goes on in Dublin than ever did in Limerick."

"But Dublin is a few times larger than Limerick, when you bring in the statistics," said some guy standing on the balcony, feeling safe I suppose from that distance.

"Statistics rubbish," retorted the guy from Limerick. "Ye can twist them any way you want. Fact is that it's not safe to walk down most the streets of Dublin. Indeed, in Dublin it's not even safe to be in your own home."

In the pit of my stomach I felt a stirring that I knew what he was about to say. I said nothing and waited.

"Look at that poor guy who was stabbed in his own flat. He didn't even have to be in the street."

"I'm afraid that's not specifically a Dublin thing." said the guy on the balcony. "That's happening all over the country. Old people mostly, though, down the country," he continued, letting the little dig get in.

"And Limerick does have its fair share of shootings..." said Mark.

"Shootings did you say?" said the man from Limerick. "Wasn't The General shot here in the streets of Dublin."

"Oh, it's a violent world, all right," said someone, but I had lost all interest. I had a sweat on me like as if I was in a sauna.

"Where's the loo?" I asked Seamus.

On the way out I met Marian.

"Are you all right Ben? You look a bit pale."

"Oh, I'm OK Marian. This damn 'flu. D'ye want to stay much longer?"

"What time is it?" she mumbled, looking at her watch. "Shit, it's ten to four."

She looked up at me and kissed me full on the lips. "We can go any time you want, Honey," she purred into my throat.

"Let's get our coats so. Just give me a minute to go to the bog?"

"I'll go in and say good-bye to the girls."

I was out of the bog and standing with our coats a half hour later and there was still no sign of her coming out of the kitchen. I moseyed in there just to see how far into her farewells she was.

"Ben, the very man." Moira was well on. "Didn't you see the flat downstairs from our place?" She was well slurring her words.

I feigned a puzzled look.

"The flat where the guy was murdered. You saw it. Didn't you?

"D'ye remember? The last party... I brought you down to see it."

I must have looked cornered. "Oh, not just you, Seamus has nothing to worry about. There were about ten of us. D'ye remember?"

"I do. I do. What about it?" I tried not to sound defensive, and if I did Moira was too far gone to notice.

"Well, was there blood all over the place? Was it a blood bath?"

I laughed. "It wasn't Moira. Sure, they had done the whole place up. Wasn't that why you brought us all down there, to see if any of us wanted to move in below you."

"It was. It was. Now isn't that what I'm telling you all. The place is not haunted, nor covered in blood. It's a perfectly normal house... so it is."

I think she was trying to convince herself as much as anybody else. "I think someone should maybe get Seamus in here? D'ye think?" I whispered to Marian. "If only to shut her up." I thought.

"A good idea. I'll go and get him and we'll be off. Maybe they'll come with us and we could share a taxi."

"There'll be no taxis tonight. I'd say it'll be shank's mare. If you get him, we'll be off."

She disappeared into the sitting room and emerged with Seamus, the knight in shining armour.

"G'night Seamus," I said. "It was nice meeting you. No doubt we'll meet again." He smiled and shook hands, nodding.

"I'd better take care of herself. Safe home," and he was gone over to Moira.

"D'ye think we'd better say good-bye to Mick McMenamin?" I asked as Marian put on her scarf and coat.

"I don't think that'll be necessary. He disappeared off to bed with Roisin about an hour ago. Let's be off. It's a long walk home."

****

"Well you'd know all about it," said the man from Limerick. "Weren't you there, you stinking murderer."

Ben recoiled in horror. "What? What are you saying?"

"Everybody knows. They're just too polite to say it. Everybody knows you were the guy who gutted the poor man in his own home in Ranelagh.

"And you stand here in polite company and act as if you were normal. What sort of an animal are you at all?"

He stood and confronted Ben. "And you have the cheek to slag off Limerick."

"I never opened my mouth about Limerick..." started Ben, but the little man from Limerick took a swing at him.

He felt the blow to his face and woke up screaming.

"Oh Ben, I'm sorry. I didn't mean to slap you... I'm sorry. I'm sorry. Are you all right?"

I sat up trembling in the bed. "No. It's all right, Marian. Another bad dream. It's all right. Go back to sleep."

"This damn bed is too small." she murmured as she fell back into a slumber.

But I was awake for a while longer.

Chapter 13

"Ben, are you all right? Is there something on your mind?"

It was Friday night and we were sitting in Neary's having a pint. Marian had gone in for a quick one after work and I had followed over when I was ready. The few people from her office had stayed for one or two and then headed off home, or for busses, or for something to eat. We were left on our own sitting up on two of the high stools at the marble bar.

"Why do you ask? Do I look sick?" I asked, avoiding the issue.

"No," she laughed a little laugh, "Not at all. You look fine. It's just you've been acting a bit strange the past while. You've been having nightmares to beat the band and every now and then I see you and you're staring away into space with a troubled look in your eye."

"Is that right?" I stalled. "I suppose I have been having nightmares... but I can never remember what they are when I wake up. You know the way it is with dreams. As soon as you wake up, they're gone."

"But is there something on your mind? Something you'd like to talk about?

"You know you can talk to me if you want to..." she trailed off.

"I know Marian. I know I can... but there's nothing to talk about. I guess it'll all blow over in time. Maybe it's something in my food." I joked.

"What I might do is take a walk up the mountains to my Aunt Maggie. A walk in the country is always good for the soul."

"That's not a bad idea. I'm going down home tomorrow. I'll be back up in Dublin on Sunday night and we could meet up in town when we all get back."

Just like Marian, making arrangements for all of us. "Sounds like a plan to me. I could take it easy tomorrow night and head down to Arklow early on Sunday morning. I'll be back on the evening train and I could meet you in the Sackville when I get in."

"I do hope there's nothing wrong, Ben. You seem so down in yourself. I hate to see you like this."

"Nothing another pint won't cure." I joked. "Will we have another one and hit the road?"

The last thing I needed was a detail conversation on this. On the other hand, I was eating up inside, thinking about it and not thinking about it.

Maybe a conversation with Aunt Maggie was what I really needed.

Maggie is my mother's younger sister.

Mum didn't come from Limerford. She was from Dublin and met my father when she was on retreat as a schoolgirl. They had corresponded for years and then when she had left college she went to work in the school in Mullingar. Dad had courted her furiously and in no time at all they were married and living in Limerford.

Maggie used to baby-sit us as kids. Before we were there she had come down regularly and gone drinking with Mum and Dad, and then after we came along she still visited regularly. Eventually she moved to the country herself and owns a house down in Wicklow.

It's a bit unclear what she does with herself, but she lives on her own down there and seems happy enough. She worked for years in insurance, working in offices in Dublin, but then about five years ago she just packed it in at the drop of the hat, apparently, and moved - lock stock and barrel - to "The Rainbow", her house in Wicklow.

The house is in the middle of nowhere and about ten miles from Arklow. I can never remember the name of the locality, but I know where to stand in Arklow to hitch a lift out to the laneway that leads up the mountain to where it is.

I set off early enough on Sunday morning, catching the ten o'clock train. It wasn't that busy for a Sunday morning and I was soon dozing as I gazed out the window at the sea, the grand expanse from Killiney out over the bay to Bray Head and on to Wicklow.

We trundled through Bray, Wicklow, Rathdrum and soon pulled into Arklow.

I met the crowds coming out of Mass and stood at the roundabout, that it should be called such a name given it's hardly a rising of concrete in the middle of the cross-roads, and was out the road in no time at all. It was an ol' fella that stopped in a 1982 Ford Fiesta.

"Was it a good Mass?" I asked, to be polite.

He looked at me as if I was dirtying his passenger seat. I felt I should explain in some way.

"It is coming from the Mass in the town you are, no?"

"'Twas not at Mass I was, not a bit of it."

That was as much as I could understand. He went on then to volubly explain where he had been, where he was going and what all his aunts and uncles (who I had previously, by default due to his age, presumed to be long in the grave) were doing this fine rainy Sunday morning. At least this was what I presumed he was on about since there was a lot of Ants and Uncs in whatever he was ranting about.

I didn't get a word in, except for the occasional grunt to keep the flow going, for more than a quarter of an hour, when I saw the shop coming up where I was due to get off. I began to gesticulate wildly, indicating that I knew where I was, that there was a shop ahead, and that I wanted to get off at the shop.

It was as if I had cleaned up the seat I had previously soiled. His face lit up in a grin and he nodded furiously.

"Aye, the shop."

"Aye, the shop," I repeated, maybe a little more aggressively than I might have had I not been seriously rattled at this stage.

He slowed the car and, with a grinding of gears, pulled into the carport of the shop. We both opened our doors and with a wave of my hand and throwing profuse thanks over the car at him as he levered himself out of the driver's seat, I made tracks up the road away from the shop.

He was calling something after me as he slammed the door shut, but I took it for a farewell greeting, waved backwards at him and kept walking until I was around the corner and heading up the hill.

It wasn't a long walk up to Maggie's and a half an hour later I was turning the corner from where I caught the first glance of 'The Rainbow'. The house was bare of leaves now, the woodbine having shed in the autumn and the veins of the creeper ran like a mass of cracks over the plaster of the house. The veranda out the front of the house had the usual two big wooden chairs and the big chunky table, but there was no canopy out at this time of year. Smoke churned out of the chimney, and I breathed a sigh of relief that she was at least at home.

Not having rang beforehand, or even checked if it was OK to call, I was taking a chance... but the way I was feeling I was a little beyond caring. I'd sort of felt that if she wasn't there that the walk would have done me good anyway. It never occurred to me that she may have visitors and might not want her depressed nephew calling on her.

As it happened, she saw me coming up the road and was standing on the veranda, arms crossed, with a big smile on her face by the time I reached the gate.

"Well now, to what do I owe this very unexpected pleasure?" she called to me as I walked up the drive. And as I came up the steps to her, she moved to meet me and gave me a big Maggie Hug, walking me into the house.

"You must be starving, you poor thing," she said as we went down the corridor and into the big open kitchen, looking out at the valley and mountains beyond. "Come in and we'll put on some soup to warm us up. Leave your coat there on the back of the chair and sit down while I get this ready. What time did you leave Dublin this morning to be arriving here at this time of the day?"

It was like stepping into the womb and curling up into a warm sense of homeliness. I sat into the deep armchair, and we chatted away as if I had just been away for an hour.

If truth be told I had not seen Maggie for nearly a year and it wasn't in the way of any of us to be on the phone every other week. I hadn't seen nor heard from Maggie since she had been in Limerford the previous year with some personal crisis that needed a big discussion with my mother. She had called it a personal crisis, but I don't think I had ever seen my mother laugh so much in her life. We never found out what it was, but Mum and herself had spent hours in the kitchen talking and laughing to each other. They both disappeared down the town later in the evening and, with a sore head and a lighter heart, Maggie headed off the following afternoon.

And now I was dropping into her, unannounced, with not a bit of a notion as to why I was here, but already glad that I had come.

We chatted through soup and a mountain of brown bread and salads and a bottle of wine she opened to celebrate my visit. I don't know where it all came from, but there was more than enough and when we were finished there was enough on the table to know you could have more, but not enough that you felt you were insulting the cook.

When we had cleared away the table she took what was left of the bottle of wine and said, "Come on, let's take this and sit out on the stage and watch the world go by. Grab a coat. It's a bit on the chilly side out there."

It was always her way to do things, as she was wont to say, arseways. She called the veranda a stage and liked the idea of inverting the notion of sitting in an auditorium and watching the stage, to her view of sitting on the stage and watching the auditorium.

The conversation was still flowing, but as the afternoon ran on the stillness of the scene began to take hold of us and we lapsed more and more into a calm quietness.

It's a funny thing with Maggie, but there are times you get the feeling that she's not looking at you, but she's looking into you. I suppose it could be intimidating for someone who didn't know her, or if you hadn't been used to this way of looking from when you were born. But I was well accustomed to it and didn't find it unusual in the least.

All the same it did come as a bit of a shock when the conversation had been light and normal for hours and hours and suddenly she has your whole mood summed up in a moment.

"Depression is a terrible thing, Ben. But a lot of it is just focusing your mind in the wrong direction and a need to focus in the right direction. It takes an effort of will, but sometimes it's the only way."

I looked across at her as if she had digged me in the ribs, but she was staring out at the valley with a distant look on her face. It was as if she was looking at the fields and into her own life and past, all at the same time.

"Fact is that you can focus on the bad things in life and get nowhere. They become all you can think about and you go round the houses just getting worse and worse. There is so much shit in this world of ours that you could have years of entertainment and only tackle the bad things."

A bird landed on the balcony of the stage and for a few seconds we both looked at its delicate features, it's yellow and grey and downy feathers and it's small little beak. It chirruped at us for a minute and then, its message relayed, flew off as if it had never been there.

"Ye wouldn't have time at all to see any good in the world."

She looked at me slowly and smiled her impish smile.

"On the other hand, you could shift your focus a little to the right and see the good things in life. You could concentrate on them for a while and see more good things... and in no time at all you'd realise that there's enough good things there to confuse a lifetime as well."

We both looked at where the little bird had settled on the railing and again, she started talking into the distance.

"It's a bit like going into Molloy's Bar and Lounge (said in a broad Limerford accent) down on the Main Street any night of the week. You can go in the door and see Macky John sitting by the bar. You know if you brush too close to him, you'll have an hour of moaning in your ear and before you know it the arse is out of your night and all you've heard is rain and bad weather.

"On the other hand, if you're lucky and someone's been nabbed before you got in the door, so he doesn't see you and catch you by the arm as you pass, you'll end up at the other end of the bar talking to Paddy Byrne and you'll have such a laugh in the night you'll want to stay there forever and come back the following night.

"Well Ben, you're standing at the bar door and there's no unfortunate occupying Mackey John's time... What do you do?"

I looked at her with a dawning awareness coming on me....

"I guess I'd try to catch Paddy Byrne's eye as I got in the door and be talking to him before I got near Mackey John."

"And if he stopped you and caught him by the arm..? What would you do then Ben?"

Thinking a bit of how often it had happened to me and how I had handled it I smiled.

"I'd clap him on the shoulder, releasing his grip, and joke with him how it was raining outside and move along quickly up the bar to where Paddy was."

"Now you've got it. He might be a little peeved with you, but no more than he would be when you leave him at the end of the night. He's a lonely old man and he needs a bit of company. Nothing is enough for him and no matter what you give him you'll only get grief.

"You can't win, no matter what... so why bother trying?"

We sat in silence for a few minutes. She looked at me and I looked at her.

"Let it go Ben. Whatever it is. It's not worth it. There's probably nothing you can do about it now... so there's no point in dwelling on it."

She hadn't a clue what she was talking about, but she was right. There was nothing I could do about it and to dwell on it was only going to drag me down... and my life with it.

We sat in silence looking over the balcony at the valley below. The sheep were scattered over the three fields in front of us, heads bent to chew the green grass. The birds twittered, and the wind occasionally rustled the trees.

In the distance I saw a car move slowly along the road at the far side of the valley. It seemed so small and to move so slowly. I tracked its progress along the far mountain, more like a hill, and eventually it disappeared behind the trees of the forestry.

"Is your mother well?"

"Aye, she's grand. I was talking to her during the week. Betty's baby is due shortly and Mum is all worked up for it. Her first grandchild."

"Isn't it a great thing. A new life coming into the world."

The car reappeared at the other side of the forestry.

"And Marian? How are you getting on with her?"

"Maggie, she's something else. I'm going to ask her to marry me. Valentine's Day."

I turned to look at her, a smile on my face.
"Appropriate, don't you think."

"Quite," she said.

"C'mon. Let's go inside for a cup of tea. I'm getting chilly out here."

I followed her into the house and only then realised what she had done. These were the things to be occupying my mind. This was what life was made up of. New life and new lives. A positive way forward.

"There's probably nothing you can do about it now... so there's no point in dwelling on it."

It was late in the evening when eventually I got back into Dublin. Aunt Maggie had left me into Arklow train station, and I was in Amiens Street by half past nine. I had plenty of time on the train to sit on her words and swirl them around in my mind.

For a dotty old dear, she knew what she was on about. Maybe it was us that were mad and not her. I can't remember a time coming away from her that I didn't feel just a little bit better about life. Maybe that was what pushed her away from it all to live as a bit of a hermit. The more you know the harder it is to live in the thick of it. Those who can do, those you can't - teach. I always figured that to be a slag on teachers, but in a sense it can also be a positive assessment.

Certainly, for Maggie it's no insult.

I got off the train and walked out of the station and up Talbot Street to O'Connell Street. Marian was waiting for me in The Sackville, and it was with a smile and a big hug I was welcomed to the bar and introduced to her new friend - Walter.

He was a fine ol' geezer, complete with anorak and flying moustache. He shook my hand warmly, getting up off the seat.

"Can't compete with the younger man," he said, winking at Marian. "I better get on home to the ol' wan waiting for me. Good night, Marian. It was a pleasure talking to you."

"And to you too, Walter," she said shaking his hand and nodding a curtsey.

"Be good to her, young man. She deserves the best."

"Oh, I will Walter. I will. She is the best."

We all laughed and as he reached the door he turned and, with a big smile, winked again at Marian, waved and left the pub.

"Quite the charmer, aren't we." I laughed as we turned back to the bar.

"You'd better not leave me waiting too long," she smiled. "There's loads of men like that queuing up to talk to me."

"Just as well your heart is taken," I laughed and kissed her on the lips.

"Mmmmm... Pay for the pints," she said, "I'm off to the loo."

Chapter 14

"I see they have another guy now for the Ranelagh job." said Roger.

We all looked at him expectantly. This was Roger. Never clear, never to the point. We could easily get a good few minutes crack out of this.

We were all standing around in the coffee room talking about the weekend and looking out at the frost on the grass and trees. We had hot mugs of coffee in our hands and a day's work ahead of us so we were in no hurry.

"Yer Man in Ranelagh."

Not everybody had it twigged, but I had. Holy fuck, what had happened now?

Deliberately I did nothing. No reaction. Not even to prod Roger. I was looking out at the frost. Let somebody else do Sherlock Holmes with Roger.

Mick rose to the challenge. "What about him?"

"The one who was found dead before Christmas."

Sometimes you'd have to crank Roger up to get the information out of him.

Jeff still hadn't a clue what he was on about. "Where was he found dead?"

"In his flat."

"And where was the flat?" asked Jeff, but at this stage I wasn't sure who was winding who up.

"In Ranelagh."

Exasperated at this stage, Mick butted in again. "What about him?"

"They have another guy for the murder."

We all looked at him.

It was out before I could stop it. "Another guy?"

"Yup." Roger was thrilled at the reaction. "Declared in the papers this morning. And it seems this really IS the guy who did it."

"But didn't somebody admit to the job just before Christmas?" asked Mick.

"A trickster by all accounts," said Jeff. "I heard it myself from a friend of mine who works in the Phoenix Park. He'd just fallen out with his girlfriend and needed somewhere to stay for a time while she cooled off."

"Come off it." Roger wasn't convinced and was none too happy to have some of his thunder stolen.

"Seriously. He'd been hearing all the stories going around the pubs on the story and in a fit of drunkenness...

"Brought on by the earlier interaction with his girlfriend," Jeff was enjoying himself now. "He devised this mad scheme in his head to get himself arrested for the Ranelagh Massacre, as he insisted on calling it."

Jeff was a good storyteller, and the boss, so we were all content to listen as the tale unravelled.

"Of course, the Gardaí were suspicious when the barman rang them. All this talk of skin and hair flying and blood all over the place was miles away from the facts, but they had to be seen to be doing something. With the Cop Shop straight across the road, they could hardly have ignored a self-declared murderer threatening all hell and damnation in the pub. So what else did they do but play along and take him in.

"The papers did the rest. The barman saw his five minutes of fame and rang every paper he could think of. Everything that appeared in the papers was complete fabrication, made up by the barman as he went along. The Cops were saying nothing. They brought yer man in and locked him up for the night. By the time the news hit the papers his girlfriend was wavering and came in and claimed him the following morning."

"You mean he never hit the court?" I was astounded.

"The court?" Jeff was incredulous. "There was never a question of it. The man was a chancer."

"And now they have the real murderer," said Roger, recapturing the limelight. "This morning's Irish Times. Fatal Car Chase in Sligo...

"He was caught stabbing another guy in his house and was killed in the car chase that followed."

I couldn't believe it.

"Ye never," said Mick. "Why do they think it's the same guy. Sure, it's opposite sides of the country."

"Not a terribly big country by all accounts," said Roger grinning. "They drove over from Dublin in the afternoon. Three of them in the car. This couple picks up a hitch-hiker in Dublin, give him a lift to Sligo and end up going for a few pints. They all go back to the couple's house and she goes to upstairs to the loo. Next thing she knows there's shouting downstairs and she comes into the living room to find her fella dead on the settee with a knife in his gut and the hitch-hiker heading for the door with the car keys."

We all stood spellbound by the story. Roger held the paper in his hand with the massive headline "Fatal Car Chase - Two dead" and a big grin on his face.

"The next-door neighbour was coming in from work when the woman ran out screaming after the hitch-hiker and he making off down the road in their car. They took off after them in the neighbour's car, the cops joined in somewhere along the way and according to the paper they were nearly back in Dublin before he skidded off the road and wrapped himself and the car around a lamp-post."

He stopped for effect while we all digested the fantastic story. Mick wasn't satisfied.

"So why do they think it's the same guy?"

"Exact same modus operandi," said Roger as if he was on Inspector Frost. "Kitchen knife in the gut."

Mick looked at him skeptically.

"And not a fingerprint in sight. The guy wore gloves all the time. Told them he had a skin allergy."

Roger was beginning to waver under our collective doubt. "If you don't believe me, it's all in the paper." He handed the paper to Jeff, who began to skim down the paragraphs.

"Well, isn't that a thing" he said after a minute. We waited. "The guy was from London, where they were investigating a similar case six months ago, in the flat downstairs from where he lived. Well, I never. If that doesn't sew it up."

We all sloshed out our mugs and left them on the draining board. As we shuffled back to our desks a weird sense of lightness began to hit me.

Reprieve. I felt like letting out a massive whoop of joy.

Like getting my Leaving Results and knowing I had got enough to do what I wanted. Like passing my Driving Test. Like being notified that I got the job in the Service.

There was a welling sense of excitement churning up in my stomach. I wanted to ring everybody I knew.

I wanted to ring Mum and Dad. I wanted to ring Marian. I wanted to ring. I wanted to stand in front of everybody's desk and soak in the glory. I wanted to tell them.

Tell them what?

That I'd murdered someone and got away with it.

The irony of it all was mind numbing.

To tell them all would be to undo the reason for telling.

This was my secret. Mine alone and must go to the grave with me. This was one I couldn't share. Not with anyone.

As the joy settled, I found myself staring out the big windows, a desk full of papers in front of me, as close to tears as I'd been since a child. As the liquid welled up in my eyes, I busied myself with my desk, unable to see what I was shuffling in front of me, and then staring sightlessly at the pages.

I needed to move. I needed to get out of there. I had to see it for myself.

"Jeff, is it OK if I go out for a bit? I have to collect a prescription from the chemist. There's nothing urgent this morning. I have the billing done and I'll only be gone a short while."

I was standing in front of his desk before I knew it and must have looked like I needed the prescription badly because he didn't even think before he said "Sure Ben, if you must. Hurry back." And I was gone out the door, putting on my coat as I went.

I ran down the drive and before I knew it I was in Phibsboro buying every paper in the shop. Over to the coffee shop and a table in the corner.

It was all over the papers. Every one of them had something, some as many as three pages devoted to the story. Pictures of the crash site, the house in Sligo, the distraught widow.

They all told the same story, from the pick-up on the Long Mile Road, to the drinks in Sligo, back to the house and the murder itself. The guy had a wallet load of identification on him and as soon as the cops got the details, they were on to their computers.

At the time of writing there could be as many as six murders over the past three years in England and Ireland, all with the same stamp on them. No apparent motive. No real connection. A bit of a psycho, according to the reports. In and out of mental institutions.

I read through every report, and could not believe my luck. I sat back in the coffee shop and stared out through the big window to the car park outside. I didn't see the people in the shop, housewives taking a break from their shopping and workmen on their break, or the cars outside. All I saw was a dead body in a couch with a knife sticking out of his gut.

Reprieve.

Live with it.

I smiled and stood up, leaving the papers behind me.

Out into the winter sunshine and the crisp fresh air of Phibsboro and a future.

A hand on my arm. ""Sceuse me sir."

A double take. Panic.

I looked around. A tall burly man had my full attention.

"You forgot your papers."

Relief.

"No, it's OK thanks. I've read them."

"G'd man. OK, take care."

Over Cross Guns Bridge and back to work. Back to normality.

Over the following days the articles kept on coming. Details of all the murders were spelt out in graphic detail. Pictures of Bert and the house where his flat had been were shown over and over. Suddenly the whole thing was resurrected again...

And just as quickly it died out and there was very little said about it. The hitchhiker was buried in London and it was hardly mentioned in the papers at all. The funeral for the guy in Sligo got even less coverage.

It had been a one-week wonder and with a profound sense of relief I began to read the papers without seeing anything at all about it.

By the looks of it I had gotten away with it...

Chapter 15

It had to be a special occasion. I had to do it right.

We had picked the ring... months before. Half jesting, whole in earnest, we had been in Grafton Street, just venturing past the small jeweller beside South Anne Street. We had stopped, as you do when you're not looking for anything in particular (or so it had seemed to me at the time... how little I knew), and browsed the rings in the window. It started as a general perusal and then slowly gravitated to the diamond rings.

Then there was the familiar purr that comes with the realisation that she has seen something she likes.

"Oh, look Ben. What do you think of that one... there beside the diamond one?"

I looked at her, and then again at the tray of 'diamond ones'. "The second one from the left? On the third row up?"

She looked at me as if I was the greatest pedant in the world. "Yes, that one." Only Marian could get that tone of condescension into her voice, but I was used to it and smiled.

"Can we go in and look at it?" she pleaded, a look of pure delight on her face.

So in we went and she tried it on. It was as if it was made for her. There was no need for alteration or adjustment. It was hers and her heart was set on it.

Then suddenly she looked up at me and looked again at the ring, a dawning coming on her. It was an engagement ring and we had never talked marriage at all. We had made all the mental leaps without ever discussing it. I don't think either of us ever considered that we WOULDN'T get married to each other. It was sort of as inevitable as old age, but the practicalities had never surfaced.

And now suddenly it had, and having seen the first material manifestation of it, we were both a little taken aback. But more so Marian.

As far as I was concerned it was a Saturday afternoon and we were out for a walk, window shopping. But for Marian, she had asked me to marry her. She was embarrassed and we left the shop, never to mention the matter again.

But on the Monday I had gone back to the shop and costed the ring. When I got over the shock, I asked him to hold it and went to the bank and organised a loan. By the end of the week I had the ring and a larger loan than I'd ever had in my life. But I wasn't worried. I would pay it off in a year and it was the ring she wanted.

A few weeks later we were passing down Grafton Street again and she had difficulty hiding her disappointment when the ring wasn't still in the window. She never said anything, but I heard the sad sigh as we cast a casual eye over the things in the window.

So I had been ready for weeks and weeks, but to pick the right moment was important... and then the idea of doing it on Valentine's day occurred to me. "That'd be a nice present," I thought.

So ostensibly the present was a dinner out in a nice restaurant. It had to be a good one now, because it would go the length and breadth of the country with the story of how she was engaged.

After much discussion in work with the foodies and 'eat out'ers in the office it was down to about three nice ones.

I left the final decision to Marian. I laid out the options and asked her which of them she'd prefer for our Valentines Dinner.

On the night in question, I called over to her flat, all decked out in my now not so new blue jeans and a clean shirt. Not that you could see a whole lot of it in the welter of jacket and scarf and overcoat I had over it all to keep some heat in myself.

Her two flatmates were out so we had time for a quick canoodle before we rushed out the door and down for a bus into town.

We walked up from Trinity College to Dawson Street and were just in time for the eight o'clock table for two under the name Morris.

Our coats were taken and we were regally shown to a quiet table in the corner. The place was pretty full, with a number of larger tables in the centre with six or eight people, all obviously out on a Valentine's night out. Some of the tables had young people, all out for a good laugh and other tables had a set of more mature people, obviously out to rekindle some of the romance into long marriages.

Marian seemed oblivious to it all. "Isn't this wonderful." Her face was alight as she settled herself into the seat and began to soak in the restaurant. For a few moments we were silent as she absorbed every detail of every table, the decor, the food being carried past on trays, the waiters, the lighting. She loved eating out and loved, even more, going to a new place.

"Oh, Ben. This is absolutely gorgeous. You are such a dear. I DO love you." She reached across the table and took my hand in hers. For that instant we were together in a way we had never been before (except in bed). There was a celebration and union like I'd never imagined and I wanted it to last forever.

"Now or never," I thought. I had meant to propose over coffee, but the moment seemed right.

"Marian."

She looked at me... and when I said nothing else... expectantly.

I stood up and moved around close to her, and knelt down beside her seat.

"Will you marry me?" I took out the box with the ring in it, opened it and looked up at her face.

She had let out a little squeak, and clasped her hands to her mouth.

I didn't notice, but the restaurant had gone completely quiet.

"Oh, Ben. Ben. Of course I will. It's beautiful. It's THE one. Isn't it."

She took the ring, put it on and leant across and kissed me on the lips.

Suddenly the restaurant erupted and everyone started clapping and cheering.

Awaking from the dream we both looked up, surprised. The clapping continued and she smiled at them and waved the ring.

I stood up and bowed to the crowd. They hooted and cheered even more.

I sat down and looked at Marian. She was flushed and there was a tear coming down her cheek. I was glad she wasn't one for heavy mascara.

"Oh, Ben. It's beautiful. I thought it was gone. You creep, buying it and never telling me." Her face was a total picture of delight.

The waiter came with the menus. As we looked at the options she kept looking at her hand and touching the diamonds.

All through the meal she moved her hand to see the diamonds twinkle in the light. Every time she'd look up at me then and smile.

It was perfect. We had dessert and coffee and, absolutely stuffed, we called for the bill.

It wasn't insignificant... but it was worth it.

As we left the restaurant, and the waiter got our coats, the groups on the big tables shouted their best wishes. I bowed again and Marian waved like a diva and we left the restaurant on a high. After such a wonderful time we figured a taxi was in order, so we hadn't got to the bottom of Dawson Street before we'd hailed one and were scooting out to Rathmines...

Engaged.

****

As they got out of the taxi Ben noticed a cop car parked outside the house. He said nothing to Marian and paid the taxi man. Still in the euphoria of the moment they hugged and laughed and walked up the path to the front door.

He could sense Mrs. Blake behind the curtains in the front room. He put the key in the lock as Marian kissed him on the ear. Just as he had the door open, he heard the gate open behind him. Marian went inside the house and just as he was about to follow, he heard the Gardaí behind him.

"Excuse me sir. Are you Ben Morris?"

He turned around. Marian came out and looked at the two uniformed men.

"What is the matter, Officers?" she asked.

"Don't you worry yourself, young lady. Just go on inside." the same man replied and turning to Ben asked, "You are Ben Morris?"

He saw no point in denying it.

"I am," he said.

"We would like you to accompany us to the station, if you don't mind."

Marian erupted. "Don't mind. We've just been engaged. Of course he minds accompanying you to the station." She grabbed him by the arm. "What are they talking about Ben?"

"Ask the lady to go inside, sir," said the Garda. "And come along with us to the station."

Marian was tugging at his arm...

Marian was tugging at my arm. "Are you all right Ben? What is the matter?"

I slowly awoke. "Marian..." I must have looked a picture.

"It's all right Ben. It's all right."

Chapter 16

In the week after the engagement there was much excitement. It would appear that Marian had no idea it was coming and was quick on the phone the following day to all her friends.

It wasn't long coming back to me.

"Ben, I believe you done the deed," said Roger when I met him on the big stairs in the office.

"Ye wha?" The heart was crossways in me. What had been uncovered now.

"So, yer making a decent woman of her. Congratulations. When is the big day?"

"Oh, we haven't set a date yet. Probably sometime next year. Give us time to get something together for a house first.

"How did you find out? Who told you?"

"Ah, it's a small world," said Roger, "You wouldn't want to be doing anything in secret in Dublin. You'd be sure to be found out."

I looked at him with a smile. "You can be sure of that. Who let the cat out of the bag on me this time."

"Sure, don't I know one of the girls in Marian's office, Mary. She'd a good friend of the wife's sister. They all bumped into each other this morning on the bus and wasn't it the main topic of conversation... How Ben Morris had got down on one knee in a crowded restaurant to take a woman on for life.

"Ye didn't really get down on the one knee shit? Did you?"

I cringed a little. I really hadn't expected THAT to get around. "Mnmmnm, I did actually. In for a penny..."

"Ye boy ye," and he was gone, off down the stairs laughing to himself.

Holy fuck, just wait 'til that got around.

Marian was on the phone later in the afternoon.

"Ben, could we go down to Balinafar this weekend? I'd like to tell them face to face."

"Oh God, do you think I should ask your father for your hand in marriage? I never thought of that one?"

"Well, you know, I suppose you should now. I don't think he's going to say no... but for decency's sake I guess you should ask him anyway."

My mind went numb at the thought of it.

"We'd better get our arses down there quick so. The story is all over Dublin already, if we don't get in and ask him soon he'll have found out anyway."

"That's great so, Ben. We'll head down tomorrow night and you can tackle him on Friday and I'll make the announcement on Saturday."

And so it was. We were on the bus the following evening and after a sandwich in the house her Da and I went down to the pub for a pint. This was the ordinary way of things for us anytime I'd go down to Marian's family. We'd head off for a pint or two and then afterwards go back up to the house.

It's the sort of man he is, Mr. Howard. He'd like to get to know you over a pint, and over the past few years we'd had a few pints in the quiet of the Ostman Arms, just off the Main Street.

"There's something I'd like to ask you Dan."

He nodded, the pipe linking his mouth to his pipe. "What is it, Ben?"

"Can I marry Marian?"

There it was. It was done. I'd asked him. After all the worrying and the sweating, I'd gone and done it.

He looked at me as if I'd asked him to pass the beer mat. Then he smiled.

"I figured you'd get around to it this year. Have you asked herself yet?"

I smiled. "Of course I have. It sort of just happened, and she said she would."

"Sort of just happened, eh? Ran out of conversation and had nothing left to say but to ask her to marry you. Is that it?" He was laughing.

"No, no, nothing like that. That wasn't what I meant at all..." I was all flustered.

He put his hand on my arm and went all serious, holding out his right hand for me to shake.

"I'd be proud for you to marry her, son. Welcome to the family." and he shook my hands firmly with me.

"Now get us a pint each to seal it."

Stunned that it had been so easy I hailed the barman and ordered two pints. Just then Alan came in.

"And one for the brother-in-law," said Dan, putting his arm around Alan's shoulder.

Alan looked from one to the other of us, a look of total idiocy (puzzlement Marian would call it) on his face.

"I've just asked your father can I marry Marian?" I said. It didn't seem to register for a minute, then he nodded sagely.

"And what did he say?"

"He wouldn't have a bit of it," I said, joking.

"Oh, that's a pity," he replied. "I sort of liked you."

We all laughed, and it was only then that Alan realised we were joking.

"Oh, you shithead," he grinned. "Welcome to the family. Mine's a lager."

The following morning Marian produced the ring and showed it to all at the breakfast table. Her mother was delighted with it and held it up to the light, twisted it on her finger three times, and ohhed and ahhed for an absolute age.

"Did you not tell your mother last night?" I asked Marian later in the town where we had been sent to get some bread and show off the ring.

"Of course not."

"How come?"

"What if Dad had of said no?"

I was astounded. "What? Said no?"

"Well, he might have. You never know. It's better safe than sorry. And anyway, it was the proper way to do it. Things in the right order.

In a way I had to agree with her... but in another I
was a little peeved. "Oh, ye of little faith."

After lunch Mrs. Howard threw it out that we might
be off to Limerford to tell my folks. Marian and I
looked at each other, the idea never having crossed
our minds. We had sort of figured we'd tell them next
weekend.

"What, and leave it for a whole week where they
might find out from someone else? Don't be so silly,"
said Mrs. Howard. "Alan will drive you over to
Limerford this afternoon and you'll have it done this
very day."

The law was set, and we were piled into the car that
afternoon, with our bags and their good wishes, and
Alan drove us the hundred miles to Limerford.

"Will you not stay the night and go back over
tomorrow." I suggested as we were travelling over.

"I will not, thanks. I want to get back to see Grainne
and be off to the disco in Hanley's. If I leave
immediately I'll be in time to change me clothes
before I go."

"And no talk of a wash then?" piped up Marian from
the back seat.

"Oh, I suppose I might have a bit of a wash as well,
the night that's in it." he retorted.

So we were unceremoniously dumped outside my parents' house and he was away with a beeping of horns and a wave out of the window before even we had opened the gate of the house.

Mum opened the door as we came up the path and gave Marian a kiss and a hug.

"Well, this is an unexpected pleasure. What brings you two down here all of a sudden?"

I had no doubt she had guessed, but it was well to go through the motions.

"We have something we'd like to tell you."

"Well come in then and tell us in the kitchen. Will you have a cup of tea?" She ushered us into the kitchen.

"Paddy, come in for a cup of tea. Ben and Marian have arrived over from Ballinafar."

The astuteness of the woman. 'From Ballinafar' it was and not 'from Dublin'. She had seen Alan in the car and put two and two together. She knew well what was happening before she even opened the front door.

Dad arrived into the kitchen amidst much hugging and kissing. He looked over at me sternly.

"So what have you been up to boy, that has you arriving down here at this time on a Saturday, unannounced?"

"Less of that now Paddy," said my mother all smiles and fussing with the kettle and plates and biscuits. "Give them time to settle themselves."

Dad winked at me and took his seat beside the range. Mum made small talk about the journey and the weather and just about anything except the reason for our visit, until she had us all with a cup in our hand and she had herself settled at the table.

"So tell us then. What is the news you have for us?"

"I've asked Marian to marry me," I said, not seeing much point in beating around the bush.

They both looked at me expectantly. I wondered what they were waiting for.

"And she said she will," I finished.

Suddenly there was uproar.

"Oh, that is wonderful. Wonderful."

"Congratulation's son."

"Give me a look at the ring dear. Isn't it a beauty."

There was much hugging and kissing and shaking of hands and the tea was cold in the cups by the time it was all over.

"I'll put on the kettle for another cup of tea," said my mother eventually. "That one seems to have gone cold."

****

We were on the bus on the way home before it all sank in.

"Well, that's it done now," I muttered as we pulled out of Limerford. "They all know."

"Yea, isn't it great. It's official now. We're engaged." She looked the picture of exhausted happiness.

The previous night had been a big bash in Molloy's where we all went for a few pints. Betty and Danny came in as well, and it was long past closing time that we wandered back up to the house.

There were sore heads all around at breakfast, but the mood was good - if a little quiet and subdued.

Mum cried a little as she left us up for the bus and gave Marian a specially big hug.

"Welcome to the family," she said as they parted. "Now that you're one of us we expect to see a lot more of you."

"To be honest," said Marian as we neared Dublin. "The wedding itself will be a bit of an anti-climax after all this."

"It will in a way," I agreed, "but since it's over a year away they'll have worked up another load of enthusiasm by the time it comes."

"They will, won't they.

"By the way. Will you give me a lend of your mobile tomorrow? Mine ran out of credit this afternoon when I was talking to Mam and I'll need it in the morning cause I'm out of the office and I need to ring Moira about things."

About things. That's as much as I'd ever get... and as much as I'd want to know most of the time.

"Sure, you better take it now because as sure as hell we'll forget later on."

I rooted out the mobile phone from my jacket pocket and she put it in her carry bag.

"Will we get a Pizza on the way back to your place or will we drop the bags and go for a pint?"

"I think it's a pizza and an early night for me," she replied. "It'll take me a week to get over that session last night. That father of yours. For a quiet man he's a great man to put away the pints."

Chapter 17

"If I had one wish it would be for a better bus service," I thought as I trudged up the stairs to the flat. The weather was freezing and I had stood for a full half-hour in the rain waiting for a bus across town.

The thought of a car never crossed my mind. All that worry about parking and petrol prices would do my head in. It was far simpler to bus it about the place, never worrying about the amount of drink you're taking, or about whether or not the car will be there when you get back.

But to be able to go to a bus stop and KNOW that there'd be a bus at the time they said there'd be a bus. THAT would be nice.

I opened the door of the flat and felt a soft pillow of a home smell wash against me. "Welcome home," it said. If the truth be told it smelled of old socks and kippers, but it was home and it was mine. And I was sure glad to be there.

I threw my coat on the settee and went into the 'kitchen' and put on the kettle. By the time it was boiled I had a fire beginning to light in the grate and Coronation Street on the TV. I made myself a mug of coffee and opened a can of stew, tipping it into a small pot and putting it on low on the gas.

I buttered a few slices of bread, eating one while I was waiting, and settled in the couch with my coffee to watch Jim having a row with Liz in the Rovers Return while my stew simmered on the cooker.

Just as Coronation Street finished and I wiped the last of the stew off the plate I heard the front door open and Marian come up the stairs.

The minute she walked in the room I knew there was something up. Within ten minutes I'd know what it was, but for now I had no idea.

She busied herself at the kitchen, making a cup of tea for herself.

"May as well tease this one out," I thought. "A good day?" I asked.

"Not bad."

Oh, oh, not a good sign.

"Here's your mobile," she said rooting it out of her jacket pocket. "Thanks."

"Oh, grand, thanks. Did you get much use out of it?"

"It did the job. All the arrangements made."

"Ah, good stuff."

"Ben?" she was hesitant.

"Yea?" I was encouraging.

"Can I ask you something?" She sat delicately on the corner of the couch.

"Of course, whatever. You know that." I was eager to help her get it out, whatever it was.

"It's just...." She was obviously upset about something.

"Yea?" I was being as warm as I could for her.

"I was ringing Moira at home today. She was off sick and I was checking was she OK."

"Yea..."

This was difficult for her and I moved closer to her to make it easier.

"Well, when I rang her number on your phone a name came up on the phone."

"Oh," I was bemused. This was truly strange. Who would I know who would have the same number as Moira.

"Yes, it was Bert Mc Bride."

The world stopped. There was a ringing in my ears. My head was spinning. I must have changed a million colours, all of them swimming across my eyes.

"What? Who?"

"Bert McBride. Why would his number be in your phone? He was the guy died in the flat downstairs from Moira. How did you have his number?"

An image of Bert putting the phone back on the bar suddenly flashed through my mind and I swear I could see him smirking at me, that selfsame innocent smile.

"Oh God." It lumbered out completely involuntarily. Like a slow train chundling out of a tunnel. "Oh God."

And suddenly I was weeping uncontrollably into my lap.

When I looked up she was still sitting there, looking at me. Through my tears I couldn't see her very well, but she was still there.

She took my hand in hers.

"You did it. Didn't you?"

And suddenly it all came pouring out. The meeting in the Shopping Centre, Slattery's, Rathmines Road, the flat. All of it. Like the gush of the confessional. Nothing held back. A complete story of the day.

Then silence.

She just listened.

Silence.

"You poor poor thing. Oh, you poor thing."

Suddenly she was hugging me to her...

And I was weeping uncontrollably into her coat, like a child in his mother's arms. Months of strain were rolling out of me, flowing into her red tartan bomber jacket.

She was patting my head, smoothing my hair. "You poor poor thing."

I held on to her like it was life itself.

"You poor poor thing."

I woke up hours later, a baby being minded.

As I stirred she smoothed my hair again. She looked down at me. There was a hardness and compassion in her eyes.

"Ben."

"Yea?"

All so quiet only we could ever have heard it.

"We'll never mention this again."

"Um"

"I've changed the name in the phone to Moira."

Silence…

"Never again."

"Uh, OK"

"D'ye want some tea?" She got up and walked over to the kitchen.

"Uh, yes please."

"What's on the TV?"

"I dunno." I said, picking up the remote control. "Let's see."